"Let's play a game."

With a teasing glint in his eye, Kerry laid out a board on the coffee table. There were two sets of question cards and two plastic markers shaped like a man and a woman. "It's called Matchmaker."

"What if it proves we have nothing in common?" Nora asked.

"I'll rewrite the rules." Picking up a card, he read, "'Do you like the way she kisses? Spend fifteen minutes finding out.' Oh, I like that one." He proceeded to follow instructions.

As usual, the moment he took her in his arms, Nora's senses disintegrated. She kissed him just as thoroughly as he was kissing her, lost in sensation. Before long he was slowly unbuttoning her blouse.

"This game is going to be an instant bestseller," she predicted breathlessly.

"Mmmm. And just wait till you see my next move."

Rosalind Carson chose to set her second Temptation on the wild, often unpredictable Oregon coast—one of her favorite places. In fact, she and her husband recently bought a cottage in the area. It's a wonderful place to write, she admits, as well as to observe the glories of nature. Rosalind Carson is also published as Margaret Chittenden.

Books by Rosalind Carson

HARLEQUIN TEMPTATION
40–LOVESPELL

HARLEQUIN SUPERROMANCE
16–THIS DARK ENCHANTMENT
40–SONG OF DESIRE
91–SUCH SWEET MAGIC
123–LOVE ME TOMORROW
175–TO TOUCH THE MOON
214–CLOSE TO HOME

The Marrying Kind

ROSALIND CARSON

Harlequin Books

TORONTO • NEW YORK • LONDON
AMSTERDAM • PARIS • SYDNEY • HAMBURG
STOCKHOLM • ATHENS • TOKYO • MILAN

For the members of the B&M Society—
long may they rave

Published May 1987

ISBN 0-373-25256-0

Printed in Canada

NORA HAD DECIDED against flying down. Driving the Buick she'd rented in Seattle directly to the Oregon coast seemed much more efficient, which was what her life was all about.

Unfortunately, she hadn't allowed for getting lost in Kelso, or running into confusing road signs on Highway 30. When at last she drove onto the wooded grounds of Oceanview Lodge, she was an hour past her expected arrival time.

The sunny parking lot contained only a racy-looking sports car of uncertain vintage and a sea gull happily pecking at a paper lunch bag. For one ghastly moment she was afraid she had arrived on the wrong day. Going directly from the session in Anchorage to the one in Seattle, and then on to this one, might have confused her....

A quick glance at the flyer in her leather attaché case reassured her. "Making Yourself and Your Time Count," a three-day John Simpson Bradford seminar, conducted by Nora Courtney of San Francisco for the benefit of the employees of Toys Unlimited, of Portland, Oregon, was due to begin at 3:00 p.m. on Friday, May 30 at the Oceanview Lodge.

Getting out of the car, she finger-combed her dark brown bobbed hair and smoothed the wheat-colored jacket of her linen suit over her hips as she studied the building in front of her. The three-story lodge, built of varnished logs, was obviously old but well-maintained. Mullioned windows sparkled in the sunlight.

Okay, the place looked attractive enough. But as she'd told the representative of Toys Unlimited who first contacted her, it seemed an odd setting for a contemporary seminar that stressed efficiency in the office. Shrugging, she reached into the car for her tote bag and attaché case, then approached the house. The side door was open. Without hesitation, she walked into a big, cheerful country kitchen and on into a paneled dining room. There a rustic chandelier blazed light onto a massive oak table surrounded by enough chairs to seat twenty or more people. Some of the chairs had been moved back and left at an angle. "Shades of Goldilocks and the Three Bears," Nora muttered.

From somewhere nearby came a rhythmic banging. Awkwardly handling her luggage, she moved carefully around the furniture and through an archway to discover that the noise was coming from beyond sliding glass doors in the side of a vast sunken room. It sounded as though someone was splitting wood out on the patio.

The tall windows that faced the ocean were draped against the sun, but there was a wide bar of light blazing through the open doorway. She could make out several chintz-covered sofas and chairs, a few low tables piled with magazines and books, and a massive rock fireplace. No doubt this room was the destination of the kindling; it probably got pretty chilly here in the evenings.

Hesitating at the top of wide carpeted steps, she waited for a break in the pounding, then called tentatively, "Hello?"

A man holding an ax appeared in the doorway. With the sun behind him his face was in shadow, but the eye-dazzling light haloed a head of thick brown hair and outlined the naked upper half of a male body. For one shocked second the body—taller than average and decidedly muscular—looked like her ex-husband Nathan's.

Then he spoke in a playful voice that was nothing like Nathan's. "Let me guess. Young, beautiful, dressed for success. The late Mrs. Courtney, I presume?"

Through her relief that she hadn't run into her ex-husband after all, Nora's mind registered what the man had said. Setting down her tote bag and attaché case, she shielded her eyes with a hand to her forehead and frowned indignantly at the shadowy figure.

"I'm quite aware that a suit and high heels don't belong at the beach," she said. "I came directly from a breakfast meeting in Seattle. However, I did bring more casual clothes with me. My suitcase is still in the car. I didn't bring it in because this place looked so…deserted." She hesitated. She had no idea who this man was, but if he had any connection with Toys Unlimited, she didn't want to start out on a hostile note. In any case, it wasn't his fault that her day hadn't gone well.

"I'm sorry I'm late," she added in a conciliatory tone. "I'm usually punctual, believe me, but I got lost in Kelso. Getting lost makes me cranky," she added by way of explanation for her earlier tone.

"Confusing town, Kelso," the man agreed. "Every once in a while we lose a tourist or two there. The Sasquatch probably get 'em."

"The Sasquatch?"

"Also known as Bigfoot." He leaned the ax against the doorjamb and began picking his way between the furnishings, pausing only to scoop a green knit shirt from the back of a chair and pull it on over his head. "Large hairy beasts with big feet," he said as he emerged through the neckline. "More human than ape, said to inhabit various areas of the United States and Canada. Distant cousin to the yeti, the abominable snowman, but gentler in manner. Rumors of sightings surface regularly, but so far without proof. Unfortunately."

By the conclusion of this surprising monologue, he was standing just below Nora, a half smile curving one corner of a well-shaped mouth below a drooping mustache, his hands resting on lean hips clad in denim cutoffs. His shirt was the same kind Nathan had favored for everyday wear, with short sleeves that emphasized his biceps and an open collar that revealed curling strands of brown chest hair. It also played up the color of his eyes.

"You even have green eyes," Nora said accusingly.

He feigned alarm. "Good Lord, how do you suppose that happened?"

For want of anything better to do, she laughed. He must think she was a lunatic. "I'm sorry," she said with some embarrassment. "I thought for a moment—when I first saw you...the sun blinded me a little—I thought you were someone else."

"Not someone you admired, I'd say. If you'll forgive the cliché, you looked as though you'd seen a ghost."

Now that the light from the dining room was shining full on him, she could see he didn't look as much like her ex-husband as she'd first thought. For one thing, he was older than Nathan, therefore older than she . . . by seven or eight years she guessed. Close to mid-thirties maybe. He had a tanned, devilishly cheerful face—Tom Selleck with lighter coloring. Not a man who could ever be serious for long, she thought.

She became aware that she had been staring at him. He was obviously enjoying her appraisal and conducting one of his own. "You don't really believe in the Sasquatch, do you?" she blurted out to cover renewed embarrassment.

"Subconsciously we all want to believe that friendly giants inhabit the woods and mountains," he said solemnly. "That way, we don't have to be so nervous about the bogeymen in the real world. That's my theory anyway. What do you think?"

She eyed him doubtfully. "There's no need to be scared," he assured her. "To my certain knowledge, not one Bigfoot has ever been seen in this area. Which is just as well. Any self-respecting Sasquatch would carry a luscious brown-eyed damsel like yourself off to his den—silk blouse, high heels, suit and all." This pronouncement was followed by a blatantly sexy grin that sent an unexpected tingle zinging through her body.

"I don't know that I've ever been called a damsel before," she said, stifling her reaction.

"How about toothsome wench?"

"Not that I recall."

"Your admirers obviously lack imagination. You do have admirers?"

"A few."

He raised a quizzical eyebrow. "Mr. Courtney doesn't object?"

"There isn't any Mr. Courtney. I'm not . . . I'm divorced."

How had she become involved in such an absurd conversation, she wondered. Who was this man anyway? She remembered that he'd been chopping wood when she arrived. Suddenly, she had an image of him slicing through a fallen Douglas fir, his ax glinting in the sunlight, his back muscles rippling under tanned skin. She swallowed, dry-throated. No matter how she tried to resist, muscles always got to her.

"Are you the caretaker?" she asked, injecting a no-nonsense note into her voice.

He looked mildly offended. "I'll have you know, Mrs. Courtney, that I'm the owner of this modest mansion. Kerry Ryan, President and founder of Toys Unlimited, known far and wide as the boy genius of the toy industry."

As he introduced himself, he bounded up the wide steps with his right hand outstretched, and Nora automatically extended her own to meet it. His palm was hard and callused in a way that was hauntingly familiar. "I bet you pump iron," she said.

He looked at her quizzically. "Every other day," he admitted. "I have a fairly sedentary job, you see, I have to do *something*." His voice was mild, with a note of puzzled amusement in it.

"I'm sorry. That was a stupid thing to..." She clamped her mouth shut.

He was still holding onto her hand, towering over her, looking at her with an admiring smile. "You've got a pretty firm grip yourself," he said. "How do *you* stay in shape? It's an excellent shape, by the way."

Okay, she could indulge in verbal fencing too. "I'm a karate expert," she replied, deadpan. "The kids in my neck of the woods call me Killer. I can break two boards with one blow of that hand, and I can do serious damage to anyone who hangs onto it too long."

He laughed appreciatively, but let go of her hand promptly. She smiled sweetly at him. "Actually, proper handshaking is one of the things John Simpson Bradford's seminars teach professional women," she informed him. "Many women still don't feel comfortable about shaking hands. But the seminar also covers more important subjects, of course."

"Ah yes. Let me see if I remember. Setting goals, short and long term, using time profitably, developing a plan of action, handling problems efficiently. Solid, serious stuff, all of it. Did I leave anything out?"

"A few minor topics." There was an edge of sarcasm in her own voice. "I get the impression you don't approve of the seminar, Mr. Ryan. May I ask why you invited me to conduct it?"

He sighed. "All this Mr. Ryan, Mrs. Courtney stuff is making me feel like a golden oldie," he complained. "Your name's Nora isn't it? May I call you Nora? You'll find most of us in Toys Unlimited management are pretty casual about names—it's hard to take yourself too seriously when your business is entertainment. You must call me Kerry, everyone does. Anyway, Nora," he breezed on, not waiting for a response, "it was Lila Armitage's idea to invite you, not mine. Lila's my personal assistant. I used to call her my secretary, but she felt p.a. carried more weight. No doubt you'd agree with her?"

"No doubt."

His smile was a force to be reckoned with. Utterly dazzling. He had beautifully even teeth, made to look whiter by the mustache that framed his wide, mobile mouth. It occurred to her that she had never kissed a man who wore a mustache . . . and that she was obviously out of her mind.

"I'm a pushover for pretty ladies, you see," he said in a regretful voice. "And Lila Armitage is a very pretty lady. She convinced me that your seminar would be helpful to my management personnel." He raised both eyebrows in an engagingly boyish manner. "You may find this hard to believe, Nora, but she even hinted that I could benefit from some instruction myself."

Nora decided she was going to like Lila Armitage. "I expect all concerned will find it useful," she said briskly, striving to establish the professional footing she sorely needed. Before he could go off on another tangent, she looked around. "Where *is* everybody?" she asked.

"Gone to Seaside for lunch. I asked them to bring back a sandwich for you and me—the catering staff won't arrive until four. We were going to take you to lunch with us. Everyone milled around until one-thirty, but they got hungry and gave up on you." He grinned at her with a roguish twinkle in his eyes. "I'm glad I'm not the type to give up."

She decided to ignore the implied compliment. "Perhaps I should get myself settled in before they return."

"Good idea."

Neither of them moved. His smile had lingered and she was having a hard time resisting it. Her lips kept wanting to twitch upward in response. She wondered abruptly what the hell she was thinking of. She had learned again and again, the hard way, that muscular hunks with wall-to-wall smiles were best avoided.

"We've given you a room to yourself, over there," he said when she began to glance around vaguely. He gestured toward the back of the room, and she saw two doors set in the wall to the left of a curving staircase. "My room is next to yours. We have to share a bathroom, I'm afraid, but I'm sure we can work out a schedule. The rest of my people will sleep in the upstairs dorms. Women on the second floor, men on the third."

She didn't like the sound of that shared bathroom, but before she could protest he had taken her car keys from her hand and gone past her, murmuring that he'd bring in the rest of her luggage.

An irritating man, she decided. Disturbing. Relieved that he'd removed himself, she put on her sunglasses, walked over to the open door and stepped out onto a fair-sized patio furnished with picnic tables and benches and surrounded by a low wall. A pile of kindling gave evidence of Kerry Ryan's labors. Beyond the patio, an expanse of manicured lawn stretched to the edge of the bluff, where wooden posts and a gate indicated a staircase down to the wide sandy bay. Straight ahead, a couple of huge seastacks loomed above the quiet water, serving as launching pads for dozens of birds. The beach was practically deserted. She could see only a couple of people poking with sticks at the line of seaweed left by the receding tide, and a small boy in swimming trunks throwing a ball into the water for a Labrador puppy to retrieve.

She wished her son Gregory was here to enjoy the clear sunshine and the wheeling sea gulls and the vast rolling emptiness of the Pacific Ocean, rather than in school in San Francisco. A frown furrowed her forehead. Although Gregory had never given her a minute's trouble, he seldom behaved as an eight-year-old should. Given the choice between this beach and school, he would probably choose school. At one time she had thought her being a single parent was to blame for Gregory's eccentricities, but that was before his astonished school counselor had announced that an IQ test had revealed him to be something of a genius.

Nora sighed, then determinedly pushed her worries to the back of her mind. The sun was warm on her head and shoulders, the breeze clean and sweet on her cheeks. She fantasized about taking off her suit jacket, peeling off her pumps and panty hose and running across the soft sand to the water's edge. She imagined the wind whipping her hair around her face . . . felt the sand squishing between her bare toes.

Her own voice echoed intrusively in her ears. *You even have green eyes. I bet you pump iron.* No doubt about it, she had behaved like an idiot. Oh well, after Sunday she would never see Kerry Ryan again. Not wanting to examine the reason that thought seemed vaguely depressing, she turned and stepped back into the lodge.

THE TOYS UNLIMITED GROUP returned at 2:45. If Kerry hadn't known them so well, he'd have wondered if their high spirits were the result of martinis with lunch. But he knew better. All fairly young—none of them older than himself—they were all too high on life to need additional stimulants. That was one of the reasons he'd chosen them. All twenty of them, male and female, were dressed in jeans or shorts, shirts and sneakers. He wondered what Nora Courtney would think of that.

Lila had told him that Nora wasn't sure her seminar would work in such a casual setting. Lila had, of course, assured her that Toys Unlimited held all its important meetings at the lodge, as well as their annual picnics and Christmas get-togethers.

Toys Unlimited was a family business, not some soulless corporation dedicated to the proposition that "life is real, life is earnest." As far as Kerry knew, there wasn't any law that said work couldn't be fun. Probably the elegantly dressed Nora Courtney would have preferred to conduct her seminar in some city conference room with rigid and uncomfortable metal chairs set out in parallel rows.

"Sorry about that, Mrs. Courtney," he murmured to himself. Leaning against the fireplace, he watched his undisciplined staff hauling sofas and armchairs around to face the back wall, where a lectern had been set up on a table.

What was it that was so special about Nora Courtney, he wondered. The first moment he saw her he'd felt as though someone had punched him in the stomach, taking his breath away. He'd been attracted to women quickly before—that was the story of his life—but he didn't usually shout tallyho and set off with the hounds within five seconds.

His imagination conjured up an image of this room with only himself and Nora Courtney in it. Flames flaring in the massive rock fireplace. He and Nora sitting next to each other on the soft hearth rug with their backs against one of the comfortable sofas—a couple of Kerry's Irish setters sprawled at their feet. His arm around her shoulders, her head tucked close to his . . .

NORA FELT unusually nervous as she sallied forth from her bedroom at precisely three o'clock. When she caught sight of her audience she also felt overdressed, even though she'd exchanged her skirt for pleated linen slacks. The people she addressed usually wore professional working attire, suits for the men and most of the women. Only a ribbon tie or silk flower at a blouse collar distinguished the upper half of one outfit from another.

She reminded herself that a colleague had once conducted a seminar in Honolulu at which everyone had shown up in muumuus and flowered shirts. *Go with the flow, Nora,* she told herself, borrowing one of Gregory's favorite catchphrases.

"I'm going to start off by following a suggestion your president made," she announced after introductions had been completed and everyone had found a seat.

She glanced at Kerry Ryan, who was sitting on a sofa in the front row next to Ted Hutchins, a rangy young man with a mop of hair that resembled carrot shavings. Ted had introduced himself when he knocked on her door fifteen minutes earlier and handed her a soggy hamburger and a can of coke. Though she usually avoided junk food, Nora had devoured both; it had seemed a long time since breakfast.

Kerry raised a quizzical eyebrow, but didn't comment.

"While you were gone, Mr. Ryan and I discussed the fact that many women feel unsure about the etiquette involved in shaking hands," she continued without missing a beat. "Actually, I've found that a lot of men aren't all that skilled at it either. I've shaken my share of male hands that conveyed all the enthusiasm of a dead fish."

There was a general chuckle. "Let's begin by shaking hands all around," she suggested over the laughter. "The right hand should be presented so." She demonstrated. "Not tentatively, ladies, or with the palm down. We aren't greeting Prince Charming and expecting him to kiss our hand. Palms should meet and fingers fold firmly around the opposing hand. Exaggerate a little, make your hand slap together with your neighbor's so you get the feel of it."

Ted Hutchins immediately leaped up, grabbed her hand and started pumping it. "Remember that we aren't trying to crush any bones," she added dryly.

As usual, she had to call a halt to the handshaking or it would have gone on for half an hour. But, also as usual, the brief demonstration had served to put everyone into a receptive frame of mind. As she went on with the program, she began to relax, herself, soothed by the familiar flow of her own words. She was constantly aware, however, that Kerry Ryan was watching her with an irritatingly bemused expression on his face.

HE REALLY LIKED the way her shining dark hair swung when she turned her head, Kerry decided. He wondered distractedly if she used electric rollers to achieve that casual, just-combed look. Or a curling iron, perhaps? More likely just a blow-dryer with a round brush to flip the ends of her bangs back. Having four younger sisters and a with-it mother, Kerry was intimately acquainted with the tools of the female trade. Including makeup. Nora Courtney was wearing just the right amount of softly smudged eyeliner to make her long lashes look thick as fur, helped out with a touch of mascara. And her bronze eyeshadow *looked* like shadow, accenting but not overpowering the velvet-brown of her eyes. He couldn't tell if she had foundation on or not. Her smooth skin held just a hint of gold, as though it had been lightly kissed by the sun, and her cheekbones were tinged with a fragile pink that reminded him of the inside of a seashell. With a start, Kerry brought his thoughts up short.

Hell, he'd known dozens of women as attractive as Nora Courtney. He hadn't connected any of them with his Irish setters and hearth rugs in front of the fireplace. There was something domestic about that particular image; it made him feel very nervous. More than nervous—threatened . . .

Perhaps her appeal had something to do with the way she dressed? The pink silk bow-tied blouse was tailored but feminine, softly draped but opaque. She had a good figure, but there was nothing showy about it. Just average-sized, firm breasts that he could imagine cupping in his fingers, a waist he could span with his hands, slender hips and legs all the way up to here. She was almost too perfect, like a Barbie doll. Maybe all he wanted was to ruffle that perfection a little.

Her voice had a throaty catch to it, a promise of sexiness that belied her determinedly professional attitude. She'd certainly put him in his place a couple of times earlier. Was that what had affected him so strongly? Her spirit? Her style? Or was he intrigued by whatever had thrown her when she first caught sight of him? He'd thought for a minute she was going to turn tail and bolt. It hadn't taken much stretching of the intellect to figure out that the guy he supposedly looked like had done her wrong. A guy with green eyes. A guy who pumped iron. He felt a surge of dislike for the unknown man. Protective instincts coming to the fore, he thought wryly. Another result of having four sisters.

He became aware that the only sound in the room was Nora's quietly compelling voice. Every member of the Toys Unlimited management team was listening attentively. Even young Ted Hutchins next to him was leaning forward.

"First you empathize—identify with the feelings of the other person," Nora was explaining. "Say something like, 'I realize it's very important to you to get this project completed on time.' Then state your position. 'I'm devoting the whole week to it.' Next, explain the problem. 'I lose my train of thought when I'm interrupted.' And finally, ask for an agreement. 'I expect to be through by Friday afternoon. How 'bout if I call you then?'"

Kerry frowned. "Did I miss something?" he murmured to Ted.

Ted grinned at him but before he could answer, Kerry realized that Nora was looking directly at him. "We were discussing what to do when a supervisor keeps nagging a subordinate to get the job done, Mr. Ryan."

Obviously, she'd noticed his inattention. Had she guessed he was concentrating on her person instead of her lecture? He met her gaze and glimpsed a hint of irritation deep in the brown eyes. Yes, she'd guessed. He smiled sheepishly.

"Evidently some of your staff feel this is a problem in your company," she said evenly, looking him right in the eye.

"I'm inclined to worry about deadlines," he admitted uncomfortably. "I call it keeping an eye on things."

She raised one silky eyebrow. "Uh-huh."

Smarting slightly, aware that several of his people had grinned at this exchange, Kerry sat straighter on the soft couch. Folding his arms across his chest, he looked at her with narrowed eyes.

A second later, she went on as though there had been no interruption. "Of course, the same method can be used by a supervisor when a subordinate isn't producing on time," she said kindly, letting him off the hook. "Just remember to begin by empathizing. 'I realize this is a rush job for you.' State your position. 'It's important that I have it by four.' And so on until you reach an agreement." She smiled. "Actually, you can even use this method on children. I frequently try it out on my own young son."

So she had a child. Kerry wondered if he had green eyes. *Pay attention*, he scolded himself. She wasn't going to get a chance to catch him woolgathering again.

To his surprise, he was impressed by her entire presentation. During the two hours that followed, she made him aware of some things he'd never considered: the necessity of encouraging workers to build self-esteem and become self-motivating, rather than just offering praise and motivation from the outside; being responsible for one's own actions first, those of others afterward; and not allowing other people to control one's emotions.

That last idea would bear some thought, he decided.

SOME TIME AFTER she declared the session over, Nora glimpsed Kerry Ryan approaching, slowly making his way through the knots of people near the snack table caterers had set up along the wall next to the fireplace. His hands were stuck in the pockets of his faded blue cutoffs and there was a genial expression on his face. Almost everyone he passed had a word for him, accompanied by a smile. It was obvious that he was well-liked, and just as obvious that he liked his colleagues. He smiled readily himself, and paused each time to say something that inevitably brought a burst of laughter from his listeners.

Her breathing had quickened while she'd been watching him. Probably because his earlier inattention had annoyed her so. That and the way he'd looked her over. Typical male chauvinist. Who was she kidding, she asked herself with an inner sigh. She wasn't annoyed with him. She was attracted to him. It was herself she should be annoyed with.

Deliberately looking away from him, she accepted a glass of wine from Ted Hutchins, who was turning into a bit of a problem himself. Ted was obviously smitten. Throughout the session, he had kept his eager blue eyes fixed on her and had been the first to volunteer comments. At the end of the session, when several of the participants had come up to talk to her, he had positioned himself solidly by her side as though he was her official guardian. He had hung in there even after everyone else had drifted away.

Now he was insisting she sample the quiche, or some crackers and cheese, or nuts maybe, and his fingers had twice brushed imaginary crumbs from the sleeve of her blouse. She'd had to adopt discouraging body language, stepping back every time he came too close, turning the conversation to general topics when he wanted to get personal. If her attitude didn't slow him down soon she would have to consider smiling sweetly and kicking him in the shins. One way or another, she was sure she could handle him.

She wasn't so sure she could handle Kerry Ryan.

"Push off, Ted," Kerry said amiably when he reached them.

Ted grumbled under his breath and glanced at her longingly, but ambled away without protest.

"How's that for the way to treat a subordinate?" Kerry asked with a dazzling smile that effectively destroyed Nora's breathing apparatus. Her legs felt as though they were stuffed with cotton like a rag doll's.

Somehow she managed a smile, though she was still running short of air. "It's not exactly according to the John Simpson Bradford method," she scolded. "But pretty effective, I guess."

He smiled again. "He's a good boy, Ted, bright, an assistant to the marketing director, but adolescent when it comes to women. I hope you don't mind that I ran him off? I noticed that you were backing away from him. And I wanted to talk to you, anyway—that was an unexpectedly interesting session."

"Thank you," she said dryly, rallying at last. But she couldn't help noticing that his eyes were shamrock green. His mustache was the exact color of his hair, tawny against his tan. . . .

"Nora?"

She blinked, startled. "Yes, what?" Even to her own ears her voice sounded irritated.

He grinned knowingly, as though they shared a secret, and she wondered if he was tuned in to her emotions. Could he tell that the rag stuffing in her legs was leaking out and she was going to have to sit down pretty soon?

"I want to talk to you about something you said in the session," he said confidingly. "About not letting someone else control your emotions. What does that mean?"

"It's perfectly obvious what it means."

"Not to me." He quirked his eyebrows in a comical way that made her smile. Would he interpret a smile as encouragement? But then, he didn't *need* any encouragement.

He smiled back, then braced one hand against the protruding edge of the fireplace, effectively blocking her from everyone's view. "You see, Nora," he said, his expression self-deprecating now, "most toy makers are emotionally retarded. It's an occupational hazard. So I really do need an explanation."

"Well . . ." She traced the rim of her wineglass with one finger, absolutely unable to continue looking up at him. He was so much . . . there. Not as big as some men she had known, he still made her feel impossibly fragile. "You might take our earlier conversation as an example," she said after a moment, pulling herself together forcefully. "You made a couple of derogatory-sounding remarks about the seminar, and I was immediately defensive. I let you control my emotional response. I abdicated responsibility for my own reactions. I let you dictate my behavior."

Feeling stronger, she risked a glance at his face. He had leaned almost imperceptibly closer and was looking at her with earnest attention. Gazing up into those green eyes, she felt light-headed again. Her breath was trapped somewhere between her lungs and her throat. It would be far safer to switch to a more general example, she decided hastily. "It's the same thing if you're driving and someone cuts in front of you," she offered briskly. "You get mad. You might stay in a bad mood all day, just because of someone else's action."

He nodded solemnly, then spoke in a conspiratorial way without any change in his expression. "What about if someone makes you catch your breath just to look at her and her sexy voice sends electrical impulses up and down your spine, and all you want to do is bundle her up in your arms and carry her off somewhere where you won't be disturbed?"

He was concentrating his gaze on her, as though he didn't want to miss a single wise word that might drop from her mouth. She felt as though she had stepped onto a cable car and it had somehow turned into a roller coaster.

"Mr. Ryan—"

"Kerry." His smile flashed.

"That isn't the same type of situation at all," she said weakly.

"It's not?" He drew his head back a little, an almost-convincing expression of surprise on his face. Then he shook his head. "You're wrong, Nora. The way you look, the way you move, the way you speak . . . you're definitely controlling my emotional response. What am I going to do about it?"

There was an intimate note in his voice now, and his eyes were holding hers hypnotically. Her pulse had begun pounding in her ears. He grinned and went on before she could even begin to gather her wits about her. "You're having a pretty strong emotional response yourself right now, aren't you, Nora?"

"Mr. Ryan . . ."

"Kerry."

She made her voice low and fast. "You are behaving outrageously, as I'm sure you know. If you'll recall, you remarked that Ted hadn't gone past the juvenile stage with women. Don't you think you're acting like an adolescent yourself?"

"Not at all. There's nothing adolescent about the way we feel about each other." He took the wineglass from her hand and set it on the long table behind her. "Dinner won't be served until eight, you know. That's two and a half hours from now. So I'm going to be outrageous again. I'm going to suggest that you go to your room and put on some blue jeans or shorts and sneakers. You did say you'd brought some beach gear, didn't you?"

She nodded, afraid to imagine what he was going to suggest next.

He smiled benignly. "Good. You go change, then walk very casually over to that door, slide it open and go outside. I'll be there waiting for you and we can go walk on the beach."

"Walk on the beach?" she echoed weakly.

"I know it's a bit of an anticlimax, but yes, that's what I have in mind."

She pulled herself together one more time. "I don't think that's a good idea."

He tilted his head to one side and pursed his lips. "You're turning me down?"

She nodded, trying to look determined.

"Well," he said, sighing. "I guess I'll have to accept your decision."

The wicked gleam that was becoming familiar appeared in his green eyes. "However," he added with a smile that was pure mischief. No, not pure... "I should warn you that if you don't agree to go for a walk with me, I'll have no choice but to kiss you very thoroughly right here in front of all my troops, who will be surprised, if not amazed. You see, in spite of the dreadfully forward way I've been behaving, I'm not really the promiscuous type and they've never seen me do such a thing in public. Of course, if I do kiss you in public, your credibility as a serious lecturer just might be affected for the remainder of the seminar. Which would really be a shame."

He stepped back. "I'll give you five minutes to make up your mind," he said, then turned and started talking to a young black woman with Shirley Temple ringlets and bright red lipstick. Marnie Brown, Nora remembered. She had something to do with Toys Unlimited's quality control department.

Stunned, Nora stared at Kerry's strong, tanned profile for a second. There was a complacent smile hovering under the droopy mustache. He really thought he had her boxed in. Mr. Cool personified. Had it occurred to him that she might just go to her room and stay there? Probably. She wouldn't put it past him to hammer on the door and embarrass her in front of his staff anyway. But if he thought she was just going to meekly give in to his mischievous blackmail, he didn't know Nora Courtney very well.

When a way out of this absurd situation occurred to her, she allowed herself a mischievous grin. With a now-triumphant glance at Kerry Ryan she turned and headed with apparent obedience to her room.

2

NORA TOOK a little more than the five minutes Kerry had allowed to hang up her clothes and change into jeans and a loose white fuzzy sweater. Brushing her hair into place, she heard a burst of laughter from the big room beyond and a voice saying, "Yes, sir." Evidently Kerry was entertaining his "troops" again. One more minute, she thought, grinning as she pulled Nikes on over bare feet and tied the laces in double knots, and he'd be laughing out of the other side of his face.

Emerging from the bedroom, she deliberately paused, waiting for someone to look at her so she could put her plan into effect. Kerry was nowhere to be seen and everyone seemed to be caught up in conversation. No one so much as glanced her way. "Hey," she called brightly.

That got their attention. "How about a stroll on the beach?" she suggested.

A few of them exchanged glances, but only Lila Armitage responded, brushing back her long black hair with a languid hand. "Now?"

Nora smiled. "Why not? The sun is shining, the ocean is calling...." She broke off. Any minute now she'd be quoting the old saw about "all work and no play."

"But it's the cocktail hour," Lila said solemnly, and turned back to her interrupted conversation.

Nora glanced at Ted Hutchins, who was eyeing her regretfully. With an audible sigh, he shook his head and turned his back on her. And certainly nobody else seemed the slightest bit interested in her suggestion.

Puzzled, Nora headed for the patio door. Apparently she had no choice but to go with Kerry alone. She could hardly stay in the room after issuing the invitation. They'd think she was afraid to venture out by herself.

Kerry was waiting for her as promised—or threatened—one sneakered foot propped on the low wall that surrounded the patio. Sunlight glinted on the short golden hair that covered his strong legs. "Why the frown?" he asked.

"I can't understand it," she muttered. "A young group like that. You'd think they'd all be dying to get out in the sun after being cooped up most of the afternoon."

"No accounting for taste," Kerry murmured sympathetically, putting one hand out to help her over the wall.

A note in his voice, sounding suspiciously like suppressed amusement, combined in her mind with the memory of that burst of laughter and a male voice—Ted's?—saying, "Yes, sir."

"You said something to them," she accused.

He tried to look innocent, but his wicked smile broke through. "I merely suggested, perhaps a little forcefully, that if you were to invite anyone to take a walk, they nix the idea. I imagine they'll flock out to play as soon as we're out of sight. They're all nuts about Frisbees." He grinned when she glared at him. "Nora, you have the most transparent face, and I have excellent peripheral vision. It was the simplest thing in the world for me to read your mind."

"Very clever," she admitted grudgingly. "You do realize that you've embarrassed me beyond belief? How can I go back in and face them?"

"Now, Nora love, there's no need to feel uncomfortable. They're all wonderful people. And there's nothing they like better than the promise of a romance."

With Kerry leading the way, they descended the sturdy wooden stairs set against the bluff. "Now look here, Mr. Ryan," Nora said indignantly as they set off across the soft sand.

"Kerry," he insisted, taking her arm as she stumbled over a small piece of driftwood.

"Kerry," she repeated through clenched teeth. "The only reason I came out here at all is that I didn't want you making a scene that would embarrass me. You've embarrassed me anyway. Okay. Fair enough. You're more manipulative than I gave you credit for. But now that we're alone I want to make it clear to you that I'm not about to get involved in any—"

"Whoopee?"

"You would call it whoopee, wouldn't you?"

"Is that what *he* calls it?"

"Who?"

"The green-eyed muscle man who looks like me."

"How did you—" She went back over their first conversation; he hadn't missed a thing. "No, he didn't call it whoopee," she said firmly. "Even he wasn't that frivolous."

"You have something against happy people?"

She was having to hustle to keep up with him. Her legs were long, but he was striding along as though he had some definite destination in mind.

He had, evidently. As soon as they reached hard-packed sand, he stopped to remove his sneakers. Tying the laces together, he looped them over one hand.

Unable to resist the appeal of the gently splashing waves Nora did the same, and rolled up her jeans to just below her knees. "Of course I don't dislike happy people," she said reasonably, as they walked on toward the water. "I just don't want you getting any ideas about..."

He slanted a glance down at her when she hesitated. "Too late, Nora. I started getting ideas the second I saw you." As she opened her mouth to protest, he put his arm around her shoulders and pulled her close to his side, saying, "This kind of idea." He kissed her gently and thoroughly on the mouth.

His mustache was as sensuous as she'd imagined it would be—soft and silky. He parted her lips with his tongue, and Nora's heart skidded in response, as though she'd stepped into a motorboat and it had hurtled her away over the horizon.

A second later, Kerry was running straight into the ocean, sending a flock of sandpipers squealing up around his head. His feet kicked up a plume of water that sparkled in the sunlight.

Nora gave a *Wow!* of astonishment. Then a shiver ran through her body. Was it sexual excitement or simply the icy water that was tumbling around her ankles?

"I think I have grounds for a case of sexual harassment," she informed him after he'd wheeled around and loped back to her side. Somehow, in the interim, she had managed to regain her composure. "You are technically, albeit temporarily, my employer and—"

"Don't worry, Nora dear," he said with a grin. "I'm not going to jump your bones without your permission."

"Jump my. . ." Her voice failed her.

He looked blandly back at her, then put his arm around her shoulders again and started walking her along in the shallow water.

She stiffened and he dropped his arm, giving her a sheepish grin. "I don't usually come on like gangbusters," he said apologetically. "I'm even capable of some subtlety as a rule. But you must realize that we don't have much time to get this romance off the ground." He smiled engagingly. "Didn't you ever see something in a store that you really wanted, but you thought you ought to wait until payday? Every time I've done that the item has been gone when I went back and I've never seen it again. So I've learned not to miss opportunity when it knocks on my door. Sunday will be here before we know it. The only reason I blackmailed you into coming for a walk was that I wanted to give you a chance to find out how lovable I can be before it's too late. I wouldn't want you to spend all of next week kicking yourself."

"Did you want me to see how modest you are, too?"

His smile was admiring. "I love it when you come right back at me. You're very quick, Nora Courtney."

"And you're outrageous."

He looked pleased. "I know. My sisters call me the Irish menace."

"They have a way with words." She seized on the change of subject. "How many sisters do you have?"

"Four. All younger than me. Bridget, Molly, Brenda and Colleen. Colleen's the baby. She's about your age, twenty-seven? Married just a month ago. They're all married now. Except for my mother. Her name is Kate and she's gorgeous. She loved my father very much, though she thought him a dreadful tease. He died when I was seventeen." A shadow touched his face, but then he chuckled in reminiscence. "He *was* a dreadful tease. I'm proud to admit I take after him." He glanced at her with a winning smile. "I'm giving you the condensed life history to save time. Feel free to ask questions."

He hadn't said if *he* was married, Nora noted. Probably he had a wife and five or six children of his own. Or else he had a nice, convenient "contemporary arrangement." It had been her experience since her divorce that faithfulness was a lost art. She'd stopped counting all the propositions she received from men who were supposedly "taken." And each man wanted her to believe *he* had never cheated on his wife, or girlfriend, or fiancée, or whatever, before. But of course she was so special he just couldn't help himself, and surely it wouldn't hurt anyone if they *saw* each other. Not in town, though, not where anyone could see them together. . . .

To be fair, she had known just as many women who saw nothing wrong with such liaisons. However, she wasn't one of them, and evidently it was going to be necessary to let Kerry Ryan know that.

A low, rocky promontory loomed ahead. "Perhaps we should go back," she suggested.

He shook his head. "We can climb it easily. There's a trail that leads through the woods back there to an open field. The residential area is just beyond that. We can go back to the lodge along the road."

After a slight pause, he spoke again in what was obviously supposed to be a gloomy voice. "I'm beginning to think you're not interested in my life story."

"I'm always interested in people," she said evenly. "Why don't you tell me about Toys Unlimited?"

"Oh, there's not so much to tell—just that it began with Money Talk."

"The board game? I've played it. It's terrific. You put that out?"

"I invented it." He laughed. "Aha, that impresses you, doesn't it? You see, I'm not as much of a moron as you thought."

"I never suggested you were a moron."

"You weren't allowing yourself to think I might have brains behind all this banter."

There was enough truth in that accusation to keep her silent. Giving her a triumphant grin, he continued. "As I told you, I was seventeen when my dad died. Mom and I decided to invest his insurance money. I made up a rough version of Money Talk to explain the stock market to my sisters. I don't mean to sound sexist, Nora, but my sisters used to have attention spans that lasted approximately ten minutes. When they grasped the concepts of Money Talk after only two games, I was pretty sure I had a winner. At first I showed it to a few established toy companies, but they weren't interested so I put some of Dad's money into printing up copies."

He shook his head. "The toy business is a funny one. With some experience behind you, you can predict what will be a flop or a hit, but you can't predict a phenomenon. Look at Silly Putty and the Hula Hoop and Cabbage Patch Kids and Trivial Pursuit. Money Talk was such a phenomenon. In the first six months that game made enough to put me and my sisters through college, and after a year we were all set for life. We're a small company—a private corporation—but very successful. We now make all kinds of board games and dolls and toys."

He and Nora sat down on one of the rocks at the base of the promontory and began brushing sand from between their toes. "Enough about me," he said lightly. "Tell me about the green-eyed weight lifter." He chuckled. "He ought to be listed in *Peterson's Field Guide to Western Birds*." He looked at her sideways. "I'll make a guess that he was your husband."

She hesitated. She didn't really want to talk about ancient history, but now that he'd told her a little about himself she could hardly refuse to divulge something herself. "His name was Nathan Bartlett," she said. "After the divorce I took back my maiden name. I kept the Mrs. for my son's sake."

He darted a surprised glance at her. "Nathan Bartlett? Mr. Southwest? Soon to be Mr. America, according to those who predict such things?" He grinned. "One of my brothers-in-law follows the competitions. He thinks your Nathan is a shoo-in."

"He's not my Nathan anymore," Nora replied. "He's married to a female bodybuilder now. I imagine they have a great time comparing deltoid and trapezius muscles. Nathan loves his delts and traps more than anything."

He chuckled. "How long did your marriage last?"

"Exactly one year. I was eighteen when I married Nathan. He was my first love—all of twenty-one. A man, I thought. To quote an old cliché, love is blind."

"What went wrong?"

She gave him a sardonic smile. "Did you ever see the way women flock around a bodybuilder? I'm not the jealous type, but all the attention went to Nathan's head and he developed an ongoing love affair with himself. He wasn't like that when I first knew him. He managed a health food store, and was very hard-working and ambitious. He worked out in his spare time, but not with any thought of getting into bodybuilding competition. Then the owner of the store suggested Nathan stood a good chance of winning and offered to sponsor him.

"I encouraged him. I didn't know he'd make competing a way of life, concentrating all his time and effort on bodybuilding to the exclusion of everything else—like his job and me. I finally saw the light one night when I caught him admiring his muscles in the dressing table mirror while he was supposedly making love to me."

"Narcissistic Nathan."

"Exactly."

They had both put their sneakers back on, and now they stood up and started to climb the side of the headland. After a minute or two, Nora stopped to inspect a tidal pool teeming with sea urchins and sea anemones and starfish. "I don't mean to come down altogether on bodybuilding," she said slowly. "I'm sure it's a worthy recreation. It's just when the bodybuilder is religiously single-minded that it gets hard to live with."

"So you left him?"

"Oh, no. I was foolish enough to think loyalty was important. *He* left *me* when I told him I was pregnant. It wasn't that he didn't like kids. But that didn't mean he wanted the responsibility of raising a child."

"You really loved him, didn't you? Does it still hurt?"

She was surprised by his insight. He had obviously listened carefully enough to hear what she was saying between the lines. She shook her head. "It doesn't hurt at all anymore. And I can't regret being married to Nathan. Gregory's a wonderful boy."

"You may not regret your marriage, but you were stunned when you thought I was Nathan. Unpleasantly shocked. Still some resentment there?"

She hesitated. "I have this recurring nightmare that someday Nathan will come back into my life and try to take Gregory away from me," she explained. "It's not too likely," she added. "He hasn't shown the slightest interest in him so far."

He grimaced. "I'm not too flattered that you thought I was Nathan."

"Only for five seconds. And the light was behind you, remember."

He grinned. "You're not going to hold the resemblance against me and let it spoil our relationship, then?"

She started clambering across the rocks in the direction of the woods. "We don't have a relationship," she said over her shoulder.

"Turned off men for life, are you?"

"Only muscle-bound men," she said slyly. "I've known a few since Nathan. I seem to be inescapably attracted to them. I've finally learned that it's always a mistake." She paused at the edge of the woods, turned and took a deep breath of sea air, admiring the long curve of the next bay. A haze was stealing in over the sea, a solitary freighter steaming along on the edge of it.

Kerry stood alongside her, looking down at her with narrowed eyes. "I could let myself get flabby."

She had to laugh. How could she not?

He took advantage of her weak moment and put his arm around her shoulders again as they started along the trail through the woods. "You have a lovely laugh, Nora. You don't laugh nearly enough."

Now that she'd told him so much about her marriage—probably because no one had been interested enough to ask before—she couldn't be churlish and shrug off his arm again. She let it stay, even though the warm weight of it was stirring up a definitely sexual response from regions of her body that had been dormant for quite a while. "I haven't always had much to laugh about." She made a face. "That sounds self-pitying. I'm sorry."

He bestowed his thousand-watt smile on her again, and her heart turned a cartwheel. "It's obvious you've had to become a serious-minded person," he said. "Not surprising when you've had a son to raise alone. He's how old now?"

"Eight, going on forty."

"Eight's a terrific age. The whole world opening up. Is he attracted to bodybuilding, too, or Little League? Or does he prefer sticking his nose into books?"

She laughed. "Definitely books. Gregory was born knowing how to read." She hesitated. "I wasn't kidding about him going on forty. He's rather an unusual...well, he has a very high IQ and a photographic memory. You'd have to meet him to know—" She broke off. That had sounded too much like an invitation. She glanced sideways at him. "You sound as though you have experience with children."

"I do." She thought for a minute he might talk about his own private life, but instead he asked, "Who takes care of Gregory when you're off on these seminars?"

"My parents. I was a change-of-life baby, so my parents are older than most. My dad's retired. After my divorce he turned their house into two apartments. I live upstairs. It's an ideal situation for me."

"You travel a lot?"

She nodded. "I've been gone ten days this time. I started in Anchorage, Alaska, then went on to Seattle before coming here."

He shook his head. "Not so ideal. A child needs his mom at home. I don't care what these so-called experts say about the quality of nurturing being the same from a substitute."

"People don't always have a choice," Nora pointed out. "Like any mother, I'd prefer to be around when Gregory gets home from school every day, but I couldn't turn down John's offer of this job. The money was twice what I was making before. And before you say money isn't as important as love, I'll agree with you. All the same, you can't raise a child without money. Gregory goes to a special school for gifted children. It's not cheap. He also has to eat and have clothes and shoes and a place to live. And I have to pay dentists and doctors when necessary. Not to mention the price of toys nowadays."

He grinned at the jibe. "What was your job before?"

"I worked at an advertising agency. John was a client. He didn't like my ideas, but he liked my presentation."

"Can't blame the man for that." Kerry gave her such a blatant leer that she had to laugh again.

Between the trees, the woods were lush with light green ferns, and darker salal and mosses and wild huckleberry. Birds trilled warnings to each other and started up at their approach, fluttering through the foliage. The only other sounds were their footsteps padding lightly on the packed earth of the trail, and the faint distant roar of the ocean. The sun slanted bars of light across the winding trail. There was a smell of green growing things, a sense of new life bursting forth.

Nora realized that she felt relaxed and unusually carefree. It was impossible not to like this man, in spite of or perhaps because of his incorrigible teasing. She felt at ease with him, and comfortable. Somehow he had managed to expand the few hours they had spent together so that it seemed as though she'd known him a long, long time.

"I've seen John Simpson Bradford on television," Kerry said thoughtfully. "He has quite a presentation himself. A fine looking man, isn't he? Sincere and honest. You can tell by the way he looks right at the camera. A presence, wouldn't you say? Like a politician. Or a used car salesman."

She eyed him suspiciously. He met her gaze with bland innocence. "He *is* sincere," she said firmly. "And his methods do work, Kerry. I'm totally committed to them."

"Uh-huh. I notice you call him John. Do you have any kind of personal commitment to him, or is he married?"

"He was married. Very happily. Unfortunately his wife died several years ago. I don't think he'll ever marry again."

"He's a man women find attractive, or so my sisters tell me."

"He's very...personable," Nora hedged. "However, our relationship has always been strictly business."

"And is there no other male person in your life?"

"Not at the moment, unless you count my father and a few acquaintances." Did that sound like another invitation? Of course it did. "Most men in the right age group who are worth going out with are married already, as I'm sure you know." She placed meaningful emphasis on the last phrase. "There are a few bachelors around, of course, but I've become disillusioned with the dating scene. I'm taking a sabbatical, seeing what it's like to be—"

"Celibate?"

She sighed. "—to be on my own without the hassle of a man around. Do you have to keep finishing my sentences?"

He laughed. "How's this for a whole new sentence, Nora? To answer the question you keep hinting at—a question that implies you think I'm probably a philanderer—I'm not married and never have been. My experience with children is limited to my seven nieces, who range in age from four to thirteen. I spent what should have been my carefree bachelor years giving away my sisters." He chuckled. "I have to admit that all those weddings rather cooled my ardor for the state of matrimony. Especially when I saw what tame pussycats my formerly macho brothers-in-law turned into. I have learned to eschew such phrases as 'playing for keeps,' 'happily ever after,' and 'the long haul.'"

"Eschew?"

"Avoid or abstain from."

"I know what eschew means," she said. "It just sounds rather archaic."

"I'm an archaic guy. One of a dying breed . . . a determined bachelor. . . an eternal bachelor." He gave her one of his charming smiles. "I wouldn't want you to get the idea I'm some kind of misogynist, though. I like women. Although I'm vastly outnumbered by women in my own family, I've always enjoyed hanging around with females, even if I haven't taken time out for long-term relationships." He grinned. "Also, I decided at about two o'clock this afternoon that I really ought to leave more time for play."

He paused so she could register the significance of that statement, but when she didn't rise to the bait he went on, "Okay, I'll confess, I've always believed in leaving time for play." He sighed. "What I'm leading up to, I guess, is the fact that I like you a lot, Nora Courtney."

"That's too bad," she said sweetly. "After my last trip-to-the-moon romance crash-landed I decided that I'm not going to waste my time with eternal bachelors anymore. The only man I want anything to do with in the future is one who's solid and dependable and ready for commitment. Women aren't supposed to admit this, but I don't mind . . . I'm anxious to get married again." There, that ought to put a stop to his little seduction game.

"You're looking for a serious-minded man, I suppose?"

"My son needs a good father."

He flashed his most engaging smile. "You aren't interested in having a good time in the interim? A sort of warm-up before the main event?"

"Not if I correctly interpret your meaning of 'good time.'"

He sighed deeply. "I'm disappointed in you, Nora Courtney."

She laughed shortly. "I thought you might be."

They emerged from the woods and stopped dead at the same moment. Ahead of them stretched a field of shoulder-high weeds blowing gently in the breeze. "Uh-oh," Kerry exclaimed. "Looks as though nobody has cleaned this out for a while."

"I guess we'll have to go back the way we came," Nora suggested.

Kerry shook his head. "Not necessarily. Look here, there's a trail. Somebody's gone through ahead of us, see how the stalks are bent back." He grinned down at her. "A Sasquatch, maybe?"

"Let's not start that again."

"Shall we plunge in then?"

"I suppose so," she said doubtfully.

She was right to have doubts. After ten minutes of floundering through the weeds, they discovered that the meager trail ended in a wide patch of flattened stalks that told a story of their own. Nora laughed nervously. Kerry grinned.

"I think we can still get through," he said confidently, looking over the top of the weeds. "The houses are fairly close now. I'd estimate five minutes if we keep going." He flashed her his wicked smile. "Unless you'd rather rest here first?"

Nora was beginning to feel overheated in her white sweater. She was enough shorter than Kerry that the tall weed-choked grasses prevented her from deriving any benefit from the evening breeze. However, she was not going to ask for trouble by staying a second longer in that clearing with its former function spelled out in such an obvious way. "Lead on," she ordered.

He sighed, assuming a doleful expression that made her grin. "Anyone would think you weren't interested in my body at all," he said wistfully.

"I'm not," she lied.

Kerry had underestimated the distance, but not by much. To Nora's relief, they finally reached the other side of the field about ten minutes later. Beyond a line of trees were an asphalt road and a row of rambling wooden houses. "Civilization," she breathed.

They paused, side by side. Nora dug a tissue from her pocket to mop her face, welcoming the cool breeze on her flushed cheeks. "The next time anyone suggests a walk on the beach, I'm going to demand to look at a map first," she said crisply.

Kerry laughed. "You might bring along a change of clothing too," he suggested.

When she looked blank, he picked at something on her sweater and held it up for her to see. Glancing down, she saw to her horror that her sweater was covered with burrs. Kerry had escaped completely; his green knit shirt had a smooth finish and the burrs hadn't clung.

"I have an idea we should clean you up before we go back to the lodge," he said, laughing.

"It's not funny, Kerry," she fumed, brushing uselessly at her sweater. "They'll think... It's obvious what they'll think...."

"Probably. Here, let me help. I remember now that I brought one of my Irish setters out here once and it took me an hour to pick the burrs off him."

"An hour? We'll be late for dinner."

"You're hungry?"

"No, but they'll all be—"

"Sitting in the dining room spinning fantasies about our absence," he concluded. "Stand still, Nora, it's hard enough to get the damn things off without you wriggling."

His fingers were busy all over her. She started picking frantically herself. "You could work on my back, while I do the front," she suggested.

"I'd rather work on your front." He was laughing hard now. "Get your hands out of the way, Nora. I can't see what I'm doing if you keep flailing around like that. You must have a hundred burrs on you. What the hell is this fabric? It doesn't want to let go."

"It's mohair." Seething, she batted his hand away from her breast, where it showed an inclination to linger. "I can do it myself."

"Sure you can." His voice was suddenly low. Taking hold of both her hands he set them firmly at her sides, looked directly into her eyes and said, "Be still, Nora dear."

As though she had no will of her own, she stood obediently while he held down the fabric of her sweater with the spread fingers of one hand, and picked at burrs with the other. "See now," he murmured. "As John Simpson Bradford says in his wonderfully sincere commercial, there's an efficient way to tackle every job."

He picked steadily, seemingly unaware that the fingers of his left hand were pressing intimately against her breast. No. He wasn't unaware. His breathing had quickened. So had Nora's. She was afraid to move in case he misconstrued any movement as an invitation.

After a few minutes, he turned her gently around and worked on the back of her sweater. She let out a tentative breath of relief.

When he finally tugged her sweater into place, he murmured, "I think that's all of them," and slid his hands around her waist.

Swallowing hard, she protested weakly, "Kerry."

"Mmmm?" His lips were against her ear.

She remembered the lessons she'd taken in self-defense. If someone grabs you from behind, strike back with both elbows and . . . of course, he hadn't grabbed her, exactly. It had seemed so natural, so inevitable, that he should slide his hands around her waist like that.

She could feel his breath stirring the hair on top of her head, and when he drew her gently back against him she could hear his heart beating . . . as erratically as her own. A powerful sensation was spreading upward from her groin to her abdomen, tensing her muscles, bathing her in languid heat.

"Turn around, Nora," he murmured, his mouth so close to her ear that his voice seemed to be coming from inside her own head.

And then she was facing him and they were staring at each other, brown eyes to green, wide, wondering. A moment later, his head bent to hers, blotting out the sky and the swaying tops of the trees.

The touch of his mouth on hers ignited a thousand tiny fires along her nerve ends, bringing to life feelings she had thought were gone forever. His lips were gentle, frustratingly gentle. Suddenly she wanted to press herself close to his body, to hold him tightly and never let him go.

Kerry savored her urgent mouth, her fragrant breath. Her arms had gone up to circle his neck and her fingers were tracing erotic patterns through the hair on the back of his head. A shiver ran through him and he lifted her buttocks to bring her tighter against his body. His lips moved against hers and he touched the tip of her tongue with his own, and felt her warm breath enter his mouth. He could sense building excitement in the sway of her hips against him, and feel his own immediate erection.

Slipping both hands under her sweater and up over her ribs, he caught his breath as he confirmed his suspicion that she wasn't wearing a bra. He flattened his palms over each warm breast, leaning his head back away from hers so that he could watch her dark pupils dilate with passion as he pressed and circled and stroked. He could feel her breasts swelling and firming, the nipples hardening as he brushed them with his thumbs. "Nora, beautiful Nora," he murmured.

Her eyes closed, she tilted her face up seeking his mouth. He caught his breath again at the clarity of her skin in the evening light, the silkiness of her hair fanning out behind her head. Moving his palms away from her breasts he pulled her even closer and kissed her deeply, his hands running over the satin skin of her back and then down over the snugly fitting jeans to explore the soft yet firm contours. No woman had ever inflamed him more. His blood was racing, his pulse thundering in his ears. He couldn't seem to get enough of her mouth, her soft, warm, willing mouth. He had completely forgotten that they were in a more or less public place. It seemed to him that nobody existed in the world but himself and the pliant woman in his arms. Slowly he moved his hands around to the front of her, forcing space between them, fumbling with the fastening of her jeans.

And then a car horn sounded nearby. They sprang apart. It was unlikely that the car's driver could have seen them behind the screen of trees, but they were both immediately conscious that this was neither the time, nor the place . . .

Nora seemed unable to speak. Her eyes had grown huge in her face and her lips were parted as she gazed up at him. "How did that happen?" she finally managed to say. "I was determined not to let it happen."

He smiled tenderly and stroked her hair. It felt like satin against his palm. "You can't apply logic to everything, Nora. Sometimes your impulses take over."

"My impulses are evidently not to be trusted," she said wryly.

She was recovering her composure rapidly. He regretted that. He suspected that once she felt restored to normal, she was going to start feeling negatively toward him again. That wouldn't do at all.

What he had to do was put her at ease so she wouldn't feel threatened and start making excuses to avoid being alone with him. Though all he wanted was to run with her to the nearest bed and persuade her to take off all her clothes; he counseled himself to be patient and forced an easy smile to his lips. "I guess we got carried away with the burr picking," he said lightly.

"You certainly did." There was indignation in her voice, but amusement too. She had a sense of humor, his Nora. She was able to see the funny side of that explosion of passion following so quickly on her avowed lack of interest in his body. *His* Nora? His mind echoed the thought.

"I suppose we'd better get back," he said reluctantly.

She nodded. "Dinner. And twenty pairs of curious eyes."

"We could go in separately as though we hadn't even met outside."

She threw him a mocking glance. "After what you told them? You really think they'd believe that?"

He laughed. "Not for a minute."

He held his breath as she looked suddenly concerned, then released it when she shook her head and laughed, too. When they reached the road, she ran the fingers of both hands through her hair and held her face up for his inspection. "Do I look all right?"

"More than all right. Rosy with passion."

That was the wrong thing to say. She looked concerned again. More than that. Worried. He didn't want her worrying about what had just happened, analyzing what it meant or didn't mean, trying to explain it away.

Take it easy, Kerry boy, he instructed himself. "Race you back to the lodge?"

Her face brightened. "Hey, okay." Laughing, she turned away from him and toed an imaginary mark. "Get ready, set, go," she called out, and was off running lightly as a deer along the road.

He let her draw ahead, then started jogging behind her. *Patience, Kerry,* he told himself again. *Don't be the predictable stud she thinks you are. Surprise her. Make her wait until you're sure she's ready.*

3

IT WAS A WHILE before she could place whatever song Kerry Ryan was singing in the shower now. Lying on her back on the soft feather mattress, straining her eyes against the darkness, her ears against the muffled roar of the ocean and the howling of the gale-force wind that had come up at twilight, Nora finally identified Kerry's latest offering as a Stevie Wonder love song.

She wondered if all this serenading was intended to be propaganda. Probably not. Kerry had surprised her by behaving more like a new acquaintance this evening. Oh, he had hovered close enough, filling her plate ceremoniously from the buffet table with his own hands. What beautiful hands he had, she thought, large and competent looking, with long strong fingers.... She sighed.

He had insisted on sitting next to her on one of the long sofas while they ate. Later, he wouldn't let anyone else be her partner when groups formed to play a Toys Unlimited game that combined aspects of Monopoly and Trivial Pursuit—last year's Christmas leader, according to Ted Hutchins.

Nevertheless, he had dropped his provocatively teasing manner completely. At the end of the evening, he'd even arranged a bathroom schedule for the two of them without making a single sexual innuendo.

She had taken her shower first—quickly—after carefully locking the door that led to his bedroom, not quite trusting his apparent change of character. When she had finished, she had quietly unlocked his door and knocked on it twice in a prearranged signal that told him the bathroom was now his.

Fifteen minutes after she had climbed into her high feather bed, Kerry had finally entered the bathroom. He had noisily—ostentatiously—locked *her* door, which had made her laugh. Since then he had been showering lustily, singing suggestive songs at the top of his not-unpleasing voice.

He stopped singing at the same moment he turned off the shower. In spite of herself, she imagined him stepping out of the stall and briskly toweling that gorgeous muscular body dry. Was he eyeing her bedroom door, planning on opening it, entering her bedroom?

No, he wouldn't be that crass. He might be a tease, but he was a gentleman, wasn't he? Besides, he had lost interest when she'd told him she was looking for a husband. Well, no, he hadn't actually lost interest; it was after that he'd taken her in his arms and... But that had been brought on by circumstances. Who would have expected burrs sticking to her sweater to set the stage for such an erotic scene?

She couldn't hear a sound from the bathroom now. She raised her head and looked at the door. There was a line of light at the bottom of it. Either he was still in there or he had just left the light on.

Between gusts of wind, she realized that he was gargling. She giggled softly. Would someone with seduction in mind gargle first?

She sobered rapidly, mulling over that word, seduction. If Kerry Ryan did come through her door, what was she going to say to him? She was going to say no, she told herself crossly.

She sighed. She might as well admit to herself that Kerry Ryan was more of a threat to her peace of mind than any man had been in some time. Nora had discovered a long time ago that being a single parent—bearing sole responsibility for another human being's life—tended to harden a person. She often felt that her business suits and attaché case and leather-bound organizer made up some form of modern-day armor designed to protect her from softening influences that might deflect her from her purpose in life, which was to work hard and be a good provider. She wanted to raise her son under comfortable conditions, and provide him with the higher education he deserved. Sometimes she felt like a hermit crab scuttling around uncomfortably in someone else's shell, but that didn't mean she wanted someone unsuitable to strip the shell away. Unfortunately, Kerry Ryan seemed able to do just that.

He unlocked her door just as ostentatiously as he'd locked it, but he didn't open it. He just banged on it twice and called, "It's empty."

"Thank you," she replied, then strained her ears to hear him leave the room.

Silence, except for the whistling wind. She hadn't even heard him open his door . . . or close it. And there was no strip of light shining now. She wondered if he had left the door open into his bedroom. Having decided it didn't matter because there was no way she was going to chance entering that bathroom again, she naturally felt an immediate pressure in her lower abdomen.

"Forget it," she muttered, and turned on her side, pushing her head into the pillow. Ahead of her tomorrow was a long day of talking. She was tired. She needed sleep.

Her mind swam with dreams, erotic images tumbled around in her head for what seemed like hours. At last she surfaced with a feeling of warmth surrounding her, as though she'd just been thoroughly kissed.

Three a.m., her digital travel alarm told her. The pressure in her abdomen had increased. She would ignore it and go back to sleep at once. She had no patience with insomniacs. You could always go to sleep if you wanted to. Sleeping was a very efficient way to use the dark hours of the night.

She tried everything. She counted backwards from a thousand, reaching two hundred forty-eight before giving up. She imagined a peaceful island, herself floating on a cloud, flying like a bird. She even practiced isometric exercises, tightening and relaxing all her muscles. Still she couldn't sleep.

She desperately needed to go to the bathroom. She was also dying of thirst. The clam chowder had been a little too salty.

She listened carefully. There was only the wind, and a faint humming sound that possibly had something to do with the central heating.

Moving slowly and silently, she eased out of bed and headed for the bathroom, deciding on the way that she wouldn't turn on any lights. She fumbled her way to

Kerry's door, which was closed, then felt along the walls until she reached the toilet. There wasn't a sound from Kerry's bedroom.

She hadn't considered before that it was impossible to flush a toilet quietly. The rush of water sounded incredibly loud. She fled back to her bedroom, stubbing her toe on the metal threshold, but waiting to whimper with pain until she'd closed her door very, very softly.

Her heart was pounding when she pulled the covers back over herself. She lay very still for a full minute, then realized she'd forgotten to get a drink of water. Her mouth was as dry as a desert. Remembering that earlier she had noticed a stack of plastic tumblers on a shelf next to the vanity she visualized taking one down, drinking a long, cool draft of water. She could go to the kitchen, but she'd have to make her way around all that furniture. She didn't know where the light switches were.

She sat up. "This is ridiculous," she muttered and slid down off the bed again. Yanking open the bathroom door, she stamped off in the direction of the vanity, reached toward the shelf and encountered warm, naked human flesh.

She screamed.

So did Kerry.

Lights flashed on at each side of the wall-hung medicine cabinet. "You scared me out of a year's growth," he exclaimed.

"I scared you...." One hand pressed to her heart, Nora stared at him, trying to recover her breath, noting with some other, calmer part of her mind that he was wearing only the bottom half of a pair of tan cotton pajamas, and that he had a thick mat of brown hair on his chest. He looked wonderfully virile and masculine.

He was gazing at her just as admiringly, obviously amused by her pink flannel floor-length nightgown, which was as opaque as any nightgown could possibly be, Nora was glad to remember.

"I wanted a drink of water," she managed at last.

"Me too." He looked at her accusingly. "You woke me up. The pipes are right next to my pillow. It sounded like Niagara Falls when you flushed. I waited until you left, and out of courtesy I didn't turn the light on because I didn't know if your door was open or not. How was I to know you'd sneak back in again?"

"I did not sneak—" Nora began indignantly, then realized he was laughing. She began laughing herself. "I've been lying awake for ages, afraid to come in here," she confessed.

"You thought I'd pounce on you?"

"No, of course not. I just thought, well—it doesn't matter now. Good night, Kerry."

She turned to go. "Didn't you want a drink?" he asked.

She groaned. "I'm not very wide awake, am I?"

He had lifted down the stack of tumblers and removed one. Now he held it under the faucet, then handed it to her.

Their eyes met. His eyes seemed very dark in the bright fluorescent light. His hair was tousled over his forehead. How young he looked.

"You look adorable with your hair standing on end," he murmured as she gulped the water. "But that's no excuse for disturbing my virtuous sleep."

One hand flew to her head to smooth her bob into place. Then the still-howling wind found a chink in some outer wall and the door behind her banged shut, making her jump and spill what was left of the water.

"Are you all right?" Kerry seemed to be standing much closer to her suddenly, so close that there wasn't even room for oxygen.

"I'm fine," she tried to say, but nothing came out.

"I really did have good intentions," Kerry said sternly, taking the empty tumbler from her and setting it down. Looking indignantly down at her, as though she'd offended him, he put his hands on her shoulders.

His hands felt large and warm through the pink flannel of her gown. "You did what? What did you say?" she stammered.

"I meant to stay safely and chastely in my own little bed, for tonight at least," he went on in that same self-righteous voice. "I figured you had all day tomorrow to get to know me and so by tomorrow night you'd be putty in my hands."

"Kerry," she said. "I have no idea what you are talking—" His fingers touched her lips, silencing her.

"For once in my life, I was going to be patient," he continued doggedly. "I was going to show you, Nora Courtney, that I knew how to behave like a gentleman, a really saintly gentleman. I was going to make you proud."

She started to giggle. Her defenses were weakening, she realized. Her shell was crumbling around her.

"But did you applaud me?" he went on in an aggrieved tone. "No, you did not. You sabotaged my good intentions by running around in a diaphanous nightgown like the heroine of a romance novel—"

"Diaphanous?" she sputtered.

"Ravishing my naked flesh with your cold hand—"

"Ravishing?"

"Ravaging?" he asked doubtfully. "I always get those two mixed up." He was laughing again, and somehow both his arms were around her and he was rocking her while they both giggled like a pair of adolescents.

His fingers found her mouth again and lingered there, his thumb stroking lightly over her lower lip, igniting a thousand small explosions in a much lower area of her body. Suddenly she couldn't remember what was so funny. She was trembling, she realized.

"Are you cold, Nora?" he murmured.

"I don't think so," she said, which was a fairly idiotic response. He probably didn't hear it, anyway, because his mouth was brushing lightly over hers in a tentative way that was driving her absolutely crazy. No doubt about it, a mustache definitely added textural interest to a kiss. She couldn't imagine how she'd ever enjoyed a kiss without one.

"I guess I'm still dreaming," she murmured against his mouth. It stood to reason, she told herself. Practical, sensible Nora Courtney would never take off her armor and place herself in such a dangerous situation. Her isometric exercises had obviously taken effect after all, and she had dreamed this whole ridiculous sequence.

"Me too," he whispered, his lips increasing their sweet pressure.

There wasn't anything basically wrong with dreaming a love scene, she rationalized. Dreams served as outlets for sometimes-unacceptable feelings, and she was obviously strongly attracted to Kerry Ryan. So if she wanted to fantasize a love scene with him, that was as efficient a way as any to release tensions and body hungers.

All in all, it felt perfectly okay to imagine she was standing in the middle of a bathroom in the middle of the night, beginning to respond as heatedly as before to Kerry Ryan's gentle kisses, her hands moving sensuously over the bare skin of his back, her fingers tracing the edges of well-defined muscles. Her breath was flowing out of her mouth in long, choppy rushes of air.

His kisses were suddenly no longer gentle. Now his mouth was plundering hers and he was drawing air from her, drawing all of her into himself as though he couldn't get enough of her, drawing strength from her so that she couldn't stand upright any longer. She had to lean on him, the pink flannel of her gown rubbing against his skin with a murmuring sound that she echoed against his lips. "Kerry, Kerry."

One of his hands slid down her back, cupped her buttocks and lifted her. Holding her firmly, he carried her into his room, leaned with her against his bed, then eased her down and rolled with her onto the mattress, his mouth not leaving hers for an instant. The soft feather mattress seemed to welcome them, enfolding their bodies like a cocoon.

It seemed as though all the tensions that had been stored inside her for months were letting go, finding a way out of her body. Pressed close against Kerry's body, kissing him as though she had known him intimately for a lifetime, she wanted to stand still in this wonderful dream while her body celebrated its relief and release. Outside the dream, yet seemingly a part of it, she could hear the wind still whistling through the cracks in the old log house and perhaps the pounding of the ocean waves, though that might have been the sound of her own pulse in her ears.

Lifting her gown, he eased it up and over her head in one swift movement. Then he disposed of his pajama pants in the same efficient way. His hands moved over her, hard and warm and caring, slightly callused, stroking and cupping her shoulders, her breasts, her buttocks.

Eventually his mouth left hers to trail a line of kisses down her throat. Her mouth mourned its loss, then began a trail of its own across his shoulder, down over short curling chest hair to a flat hard nipple that hardened even more as her tongue touched it to life.

It had to be a dream. She tried to convince herself it couldn't possibly be reality. Nora Courtney making love to a man she hadn't even met before this time yesterday? If this was reality she'd be shocked at herself, wouldn't she? Maybe. And then again, maybe it was time she indulged herself in something that was purely enjoyable. Kerry was right about her—she was much too serious. What harm could it possibly do to indulge in a lighthearted interlude?

"Nora?" He was over her, braced on both hands, his mouth tough and stern, his eyes blazing green fire in the light that still poured over them from the bathroom.

Her hands reached for his face, touched lightly, stroked down to his jaw, then fell away. She smiled and opened her body to him, feeling him sink into her. She watched his face, loving the way his mouth relaxed and his eyes widened with profound pleasure as he entered her and began to thrust gently, rhythmically, timing himself to her own lifting, rocking motions.

"This is some dream," she whispered.

His eyes laughed at her, then narrowed, as his movements slowed and he concentrated on his own inner processes. "Nora, darling Nora," he groaned.

She lifted her legs and wrapped them around him, holding him still. "Wait," she urged him, feeling her own forces gathering themselves for one great explosion.

A heartbeat, and the indescribable sweetness that was like thick golden honey surging from every vein in her body toward the area between her thighs became an urgent wave. It picked her up and pressed her against Kerry's hard, hard body for one breathless, jagged, motionless moment before racing on to leave her gasping beneath him on the bed.

Before she could even catch her breath he was lifting her to him again, his hands urging her closer and closer as though he wanted her to become a part of him as he was a part of her. And then he was moving more rapidly, but just as rhythmically. Unbelievably, she was quickening again, pressure building up inside her to match the pressure he was exerting. The two of them rose and fell together, until the pressure exploded into another wave that rolled over them and away.

Nora was warm, and far more relaxed than she had any business being. She knew she should be worried by her own behavior, anxiously working out why she had allowed such a thing to happen, how she could possibly have allowed such a thing to happen. But she didn't want to worry about it, not tonight, not when Kerry was holding her comfortably, warmly, intimately, his breath feathering against her face. Relaxation stole through her entire body, softening the grip of her arms around Kerry, pressing her spine down into the soft feather mattress, tugging her eyes closed.

"Kerry," she murmured.

"Nora?" He sounded fuzzy with sleep, but prepared to become alert. If she insisted, she thought, he would fight against the sleep that was overcoming him. Her hands stroked his back gently, letting him know she didn't require the effort from him, and then she let the delicious languor take over her own body and waft her away into sleep.

SHE AWOKE to the high-pitched beeping of her travel alarm. Seven o'clock. The sun was streaming in through the window, warming her closed eyelids. How could that be, Nora wondered, as she remembered that she was staying at Oceanview Lodge on the Oregon coast. Her room faced the Pacific, which was on the west side of any map ever printed. Wasn't the sun supposed to rise in the east?

Her eyes shot open and she sat upright and hurled the covers to one side, looking around wildly. The sun was streaming in because she wasn't in her own bedroom, she was on the other side of the house, in Kerry Ryan's room. Kerry wasn't there, but she hadn't been aware of him leaving. He must have brought her alarm clock in so she wouldn't oversleep. Why hadn't he simply awakened her himself?

Mulling the question, she became convinced that he'd left because he regretted making love to her. He didn't want to face her in the bright light of morning.

She laughed shortly at herself. "Women," she muttered, "always ready to believe the worst."

Kerry wasn't in the bathroom, either, but he had been there recently; steam coated the mirror, and the shower stall was wet. He'd put out clean towels for her. That was thoughtful of him.

She should probably go into Kerry's room and make his bed, she thought after she'd made her own. Apparently there wasn't any maid service. But if someone came in while she was in there—someone who wasn't Kerry—she'd sure hate to have to explain her presence. Besides, she was supposed to be a liberated woman. Let Kerry Ryan make his own bed.

Everyone except Kerry was at breakfast when she finally emerged from her room. They called cheery good-mornings to her as she crossed the vast living room. Ted Hutchins was sitting at the head of the long table, presiding over a huge coffee maker. He grinned at her as she took the only seat available, about halfway down the table to his right. "Coffee?" he asked.

She nodded, and he passed a cup down to her. Several conversations, interrupted by her arrival, had started up again. Marnie, sitting next to Nora, finished describing a bird she'd seen on a tree out front the previous day. "Kerry said it was a red-breasted sapsucker," she told Nora. "Was he putting me on?"

"I don't think so," Nora said carefully. "At least there is such a bird. It's a type of woodpecker." She hesitated. "Where is Kerry... Mr. Ryan?" she asked.

Lila answered. "He got called away early, around six, I guess. Family emergency."

One of the catering crew, a short plump gray-haired man who had told Nora the previous evening that she had the prettiest smile in the world, poked his head around the doorjamb. Seeing Nora, he quickly brought her a plate of sausages and scrambled eggs.

She forced a smile. "What kind of emergency?" she asked, hoping her voice sounded casual.

Lila smiled vaguely. "Something to do with one of his brothers-in-law. He didn't go into details."

Nora gazed at her plate in silence, wondering if anyone would notice if she didn't eat a bite. Was it paranoid to think Kerry might have made up the story about his brother-in-law? In a genuine emergency, surely he would have woken her up, explained, said something, anything, that would let her know he wasn't just running out after a one-night stand.

Probably she would never know if there really had been an emergency. It dawned on her that she didn't know Kerry well enough to know if he was usually truthful or a congenital liar. And if she didn't know him, what the hell was she doing going to bed with him last night? She hadn't thought, that was the trouble. And now Kerry Ryan was gone, leaving her to feel totally humiliated.

As Marnie started in on a long, involved question about yesterday's seminar, Nora forced herself to eat half a sausage and a forkful of scrambled eggs. At least no one else knew the depth of her humiliation. Somehow she would have to pretend nothing had happened so she could keep it that way.

It was a very long day. Only discipline got her through it. Discipline and the fact that she knew her subject so well she could have lectured in her sleep. All that was missing was her usual enthusiasm. Somehow, 'Handling stressful disagreements,' 'Learning positive aggression,' and 'Presenting ideas and suggestions persuasively,' didn't seem as fascinating to her as usual. She felt used and abused and embarrassingly naive. She had really liked Kerry Ryan. She would not have gone to bed with a man she didn't like, didn't instinctively trust.

Dumb, Nora.

After dinner, the group invited her to accompany them to a bar in Seaside. Deciding she would probably lie awake castigating herself if she stayed at the lodge, she accepted the invitation and tried to enjoy and share in the high spirits of the Toys Unlimited employees.

"It's too bad Kerry isn't here," Ted Hutchins said as he danced her around the floor in a spirited Texas two-step. "Kerry loves western music."

Nora risked a question. "Was there really an emergency?"

Ted chuckled as he escorted her back to their table. "With Kerry it's hard to tell. Sometimes he has himself paged out of sales meetings if he's bored or he has a hot date—" He broke off and blushed furiously, evidently just realizing who he was talking to. "I didn't mean that *you* are boring," he said earnestly. "I really got into all that stuff about developing a plan of action, and proper thought patterns and the steps to success. Kerry probably did have an emergency, this time."

"Probably," Nora murmured, sorry she'd asked. Poor Ted was getting very flustered, wondering if he'd said more than he should have, wondering if he'd offended her.

The jukebox was playing again. "Let's dance some more, shall we?" she suggested brightly, and was rewarded by an eager smile as Ted leaped to his feet and grabbed her hand.

She was going to survive this evening, she told herself as Ted swung her around wildly. She was going to sleep well tonight and get through the morning sessions and fly home to San Francisco and try to forget she had ever thought a lighthearted interlude with Kerry Ryan might be fun.

WHEN ANYONE ASKED HER which she liked best of the many cities she'd visited, Nora always answered, without hesitating, San Francisco. She had been born in San Francisco, had gone to school and grown up there, and hoped to spend the rest of her life there. She liked to tell everyone she met that one of the few things San Franciscans ever agreed on was that they wouldn't want to live anywhere else.

Whenever she had been away, the dynamic and colorful city seemed to welcome her home. She loved every one of the roller-coaster hills, and considered the view of the bay and the Golden Gate bridge the best sight in the world, whether she looked at it at night, or in daytime with fog swirling in from the Pacific. She also loved the colorful and confused architecture, the flower stands on the street corners, the rackety, wonderful, heart-in-your-mouth-and-hang-on-tight-cable cars, and the entire sophisticated, broad-minded, fun-loving population that was an alphabet soup of Anglo-Saxons, Italians, Hispanics, Japanese and Chinese and others, all mixed together to form a spirit that made the city sing.

After paying off the cab she'd taken from the airport and walking up the front steps of her parents' house in the crisp air of Sunday evening, she began to feel that she would not only survive the humiliation of her weekend in Oregon, but would do so with the anticipation of happiness. It was good to be home. She considered herself lucky to live in this wonderful old Victorian house that had been lovingly restored by her parents and painted coral to contrast effectively with its café-au-lait and powder-blue neighbors.

There was no answer when she knocked on the front door. That wasn't unusual of course; her parents often moved up to her apartment on the day she was expected home, so that they could air it out and make it welcoming for her. "Hey, Gregory," she called as she hauled her baggage up the interior stairs.

Her door didn't fly open. Gregory could be watching educational television, of course, or he might have gone up to his attic bedroom to look through his beloved telescope. Setting down her luggage, Nora fumbled her key into the lock and called, "Hey, where's my welcoming committee?" as the door swung open.

"Here I am," Kerry Ryan said.

He was leaning negligently in the doorway that led to her small living room, dressed in a striped pink shirt with a narrow white tie, and white denim pants that fitted his lean hips as though he'd been poured into them. He beamed at her. "It's about time you got here," he said. "We were beginning to worry."

Nora gaped at him as though he were an apparition that had materialized through the walls of the tiny entrance foyer of her apartment. A couple of times she started to speak, couldn't, and had to swallow.

"I'll bet you're surprised to see me," he said brightly. "Lucky for me you're listed in the phone book."

"Mom, you're home!" Belatedly, Gregory appeared from behind Kerry, pushing past him to fling his skinny young body into Nora's arms. Squatting on her heels, she returned his exuberant hug, the two of them almost toppling over in their enthusiasm. She felt a surge of love for him. He had a stranglehold on her neck. She wanted him never to let go. But eventually he did.

"Oh, I missed you, Gregory Courtney," she told him as she planted a kiss on the freckles that bridged his nose and smoothed his spiky dark bangs—he had a habit of tugging at them when he was studying something. His hair smelled vaguely herbal. Grandma's shampoo. Skinny or not, he looked wonderful to her in his black "Halley's Comet" T-shirt and blue jeans and Adidas, his thin clever face and green eyes alight with pleasure.

"Where's Gran?" she asked. She didn't think her sometimes absentminded mother would leave Gregory alone with a stranger, but everything seemed so suddenly topsy-turvy she thought she'd better make sure.

"In the kitchen, of course," Gregory said as though women didn't belong anywhere else, an attitude Lillian Courtney would probably agree with.

"Grandpa up here too?" Nora asked.

He nodded. "Watching 60 Minutes in your office and cheering for Mike Wallace."

"Is everything A-okay with you?" she asked, leaning her head back so she could look directly into his intelligent eyes.

"Absolutely," he answered, nodding solemnly.

This greeting and its response was their own private code, used if anyone else was present. If Gregory had answered okay, or sure, or merely yes, it would have meant he was unhappy about something and needed to talk in private. "Absolutely," meant there wasn't a cloud on his horizon.

There was one on hers. She hugged Gregory one more time, mostly because she wanted to, but also to give her time to adjust to the shock of Kerry Ryan's presence. Then she looked up into the pair of green eyes that were almost twins to her son's.

"Yes, I am surprised to see you," she answered finally, getting to her feet.

Kerry's smile disappeared as though a light had been switched off, and he slanted a sideways glance at Gregory that was evidently meant to convey despair. "She's frosted, isn't she?"

Gregory's brow furrowed, which made him look a lot like Nora's father, another worrier. Between the two of them, they managed to worry about everything and everybody in the world. "Mom doesn't like surprises, Kerry," he confided.

"Kerry?" Nora queried. "Shouldn't it be Mr. Ryan?"

"I insisted," Kerry said. "I hate formality, remember?" He was still looking at Gregory. "She doesn't like any kind of surprises?"

Gregory frowned thoughtfully. "I guess she doesn't mind if they're happy ones."

"She doesn't look upon me as a happy surprise then?"

"I guess not."

"I'm crushed."

"Shattered?"

"Pulverized."

The two pairs of green eyes looked at her mournfully. Somehow Kerry had established a teasing relationship with her son that no one else had ever attempted. "How long have you been here?" she asked him.

"About two hours. Gregory and I got to studying the sun on a projection screen he hooked up to his telescope. Fascinating. We lost track of time, I'm afraid. Your mother insisted I should stay for dinner," he added with a winning smile. "What a lovely woman she is, everything a mother should be. I take back what I said about Gregory needing you at home—he's obviously getting first-rate care." He grinned. "We're having baked chicken, with little red potatoes cooked around it, beets and green beans on the side, and my favorite salad— spinach with sliced banana and chunks of orange."

"It appears you are loved by one and all," Nora said dryly.

"What's not to love?" he asked.

She looked at him quizzically, trying not to let herself be drawn in by the potent charm of his smiling green eyes. "Your disappearing act wasn't too lovable."

"I'll go tell Gran you're ready for dinner," Gregory said, manfully lifting Nora's tote bag and dragging her suitcase toward the hall, displaying a tact he wasn't usually capable of. "Kerry says I've got your cheekbones, Mom," he added over his shoulder. He giggled. "He also says I have *his* eyes."

Nora looked at Kerry with exasperation. "What a thing to tell an eight-year-old boy. What if he repeats it to someone? Can you guess what they'd think?"

He grinned and nodded, not at all contrite. Nora sighed.

"You didn't get my note?" Kerry asked.

"There was hardly time for the mail to deliver—"

"I left a note on my pillow, explaining that Jordan Lambert, my sister Bridget's husband, was involved in an automobile accident."

About to argue that he'd done no such thing, Nora remembered flinging back the covers on his bed and shooting out of the room. She hadn't gone back in after deciding to let him make his own bed.

"I told you that Bridget and Jordan live in San Francisco, didn't I?" Kerry said with a frown. "On Russian Hill?"

"No, you didn't."

"Remiss of me. You'll be delighted to hear that I often visit them," he added with a meaningful smile. "Anyway, the two of them own twin Porsches, poppy red in color. They decided over an early breakfast in their apartment yesterday morning that it would be stupendous fun to race the cars down Lombard Street."

Nora was horrified. "Not the crooked part?"

"Every single switchback. I understand that at one point Jordan's car became airborne. When he landed, he and the car were upside down. The car was totaled. When Bridget called me at dawn she implied that he'd totaled himself, which is why I left so hurriedly. My sisters tend to hysterics at the best of times. At the worst of times they come unglued."

"Is he okay?"

"He was lucky. He got off with a concussion. He has a singularly hard head. He'll be fine in a couple of days."

He smiled at her. "Thank you for your concern, Nora. Many people would have condemned the act before worrying about the results. You have a kind heart, as well as numerous other praiseworthy attributes."

He was looking at her so lovingly that her breathing was becoming affected. "I didn't see any note," she said tersely, in order to reestablish some distance between them. "No one else knew where you'd gone either."

"They didn't need to. I prefer not to let my staff know every time one of my family messes up. But you surely didn't think I'd take off without a word to you?" He studied her face when she didn't answer right away. "You *did* think that's what I'd done."

She nodded.

"I would never do that, Nora." He took a step toward her with the obvious intention of taking her in his arms.

Suddenly flustered, Nora bent to pick up her attaché case. "We don't have to take root in the foyer," she said. "We can at least go in and have a cup of coffee or—"

"Your mother just made a pot of tea," he interrupted, following her into the living room. "Darjeeling. My favorite kind."

"I'm so glad for you." She set her briefcase down, turning in time to see him wince.

"Why am I getting the idea you aren't overjoyed by my presence, Nora?" he asked after a moment's silence.

"I'm overwhelmed," she admitted. "I didn't expect to even see you again, so it's something of a surprise to find you've moved in here."

"My mother says I'm inclined to be a bit brash," he admitted with a sigh. "I'm sorry, Nora, perhaps I'd better forego dinner."

"You'll do nothing of the sort," Lillian Courtney said, bustling into the room with a tray loaded with Nora's ornate silver tea service, her salt-and-pepper hair curling around her smiling face, a ruffled apron tied around her sturdy waist. Nora frowned. That silver hadn't seen the light of day since her Aunt Amy gave it to her as a wedding present. Kerry obviously rated.

"I had quite a time mixing up that honey dressing you told me about, Kerry," Lillian informed him. "I had to warm the honey before it would mix with the oil and lemon and salt and then I had to cool it down again. Least you can do is stay and try it, tell me if it tastes right."

She put the tray down and came over to Nora to give her a hug. "Welcome home, darling. Everything's just fine. Your mail's on your desk, and I saved the Sunday papers for you. Mr. Bradford called. He wants you to have dinner with him on Friday, June 6. He'll pick you up at 6:30. He'll be out of town until then. Denver, Colorado, he said. I think. Or was it San Diego?"

Pausing for breath, she beamed at her daughter and went on. "Whatever. You look lovely, Nora. Is that a new blouse? It goes well with your suit. Such a pretty lemon color. I thought I'd cook dinner up here for a change so I could try out your new microwave. Hope that's okay with you. It's a new chicken recipe. I'll give it to you if it works out."

Turning away to pour her tea, she added with a puckish grin for Kerry. "Don't pay any attention to

Nora until she's been home an hour or so. She's always grouchy when she comes off an airplane."

"She's grouchy to me even when there's no airplane involved," Kerry said mournfully.

"That doesn't mean she doesn't like you," Gregory explained, coming in with a silver cream pitcher. "You put this in the kitchen sink with the dirty pots, Gran," he commented. "I washed it off." With a grin for Kerry, he added, "It's when Mom's really polite that you have to watch out. She can 'I beg your pardon' and 'Is that really so?' a person to death."

"So what do you call, 'I'm so glad for you,' and 'It appears you are loved by one and all'?" Kerry asked him, mimicking Nora's tone of voice with uncanny skill and making Lillian laugh out loud.

"I'm going to beat all three of your heads together if you go on acting as if I'm not here," Nora said, but resigned amusement was clear in her voice. It was impossible to stay mad at Kerry Ryan when he was present, especially when it was obvious that her son and her mother were both charmed by him.

So was her father, she discovered when Charlie Courtney finally came out of her tiny office. Nora's father was a tall balding man, whose imposing presence covered up a basic shyness. Nora always thought he looked more like the maitre d' of a first-class restaurant than a retired building contractor. Right now he was indulging in what his wife called "chuntering"—a sort of hostile sotto voce mutter that meant he was upset about something. "What do you think of these foreigners buying up so much of California?" he demanded of Kerry in a disgusted tone of voice after he'd hugged Nora.

"I guess we all came here from somewhere else," Kerry said diplomatically.

"Yes, well I suppose that's right," Charlie admitted with an air of surprise. Nora considered reminding him that Kerry didn't share his concern because Kerry was an Oregonian, but Kerry's statement had obviously cheered her father up and she didn't want to risk depressing him again.

"Isn't this cozy?" Kerry said when they were all seated around Nora's sheet glass coffee table. "I like your apartment, Nora, even though it doesn't match the house. At first it was a bit surprising. . . ."

"Surprising is the least of it," Charlie grumbled. "I feel as though I'm going through a time warp every time I come up here. All the effort I put into meticulous nineteenth-century restoration and then the prodigal returns to fill half of it with high-tech glass and steel."

"I bought this furniture to go with a solar-heated condo," Nora pointed out defensively. "And anyway, it looks great in here. The contrast in periods is so unexpected that it works."

"And you have excellent taste," Kerry murmured soothingly. "I've always thought contemporary furnishings were sterile, but you've managed to give them a certain warmth . . . which shouldn't surprise me."

She flashed him a warning glance designed to alert him to the fact that her father could read double entendres at twenty paces, but he didn't take the hint. "The white silk lilies in the crystal vase on your white wood dining table, for example," he continued. "With anyone else one would imagine a certain . . . well, one hesitates to say frigidity, perhaps colorless personality would be a better choice of words . . . but the number of lilies, the sheer extravagance of the display lends instead an air of . . . generosity."

Lillian was nodding solemnly.

"You agree with me, don't you, Lillian?"

First names all around. He was a fast worker.

"I'm not sure I even understand the question," Lillian admitted with an apologetic shrug. "But I've been telling Nora for years that she needs some color in her life. . . ."

"And here I am," Kerry supplied when Lillian paused, making her laugh again.

Charlie didn't laugh, Nora noted. Instead, her father's blue eyes narrowed behind his dark-rimmed glasses and he looked at Kerry with suddenly intense interest, one hand smoothing his sparse gray hair across the top of his head. Nora wondered if he was for or against. With Charles Courtney you sometimes couldn't be sure.

Probably *for*, she decided a little while later. All through dinner—which was a great success even though Lillian didn't remember to serve the gravy until all the potatoes and biscuits were gone—Kerry held all their attention with one humorous story after another. No one even remembered to ask Nora how her seminars had gone until they were halfway through the chocolate mousse. And as soon as she said, "Fine," Charlie asked Kerry another question about the toy industry and he was off again.

Not that Nora really minded Kerry hogging the limelight. He was certainly an interesting conversationalist. He told them all about the genesis of Monopoly and how Charles Darrow, its inventor and an engineering sales rep who made jigsaw puzzles as a sideline, had named the properties after actual streets in Atlantic City because he had fond memories of a vacation there. Then he went on to tell them about his own invention of Money Talk and the fact that it had succeeded while a previous game called Bulls and Bears, invented by Charles Darrow, had gone nowhere.

Nora had to admit to herself that she was impressed by Kerry's philosophy. "The right toy at the right age can guide a child for life," he asserted. "Children need quality play. The late Marvin Glass, the most successful free-lance toy inventor in the U.S. said, 'Play allows a child to explore unreality and then return to the real world.' And of course, adults need playtime too. To quote an old saw, the only difference between men and boys is the price of their toys." He held up one hand to forestall Nora's automatic protest. "I know that sounds sexist, Nora," he admitted with a grin. "But if you say adults and children there's nothing to rhyme with toys."

"I'm familiar with Toys Unlimited," Charlie said. "Seems to me a spokesperson for your company was quoted pretty extensively in a recent *Newsweek* article about product safety."

"That was me," Kerry told him. "As far as I'm concerned, safety goes hand in hand with quality."

"What about war toys?" Lillian asked, pursuing one of her pet peeves.

"*Gran*," Gregory protested, but she paid no attention to him.

"For a while you didn't see kids with toy guns and tanks," Lillian said, looking at Kerry challengingly, "but lately I've noticed a lot of Star Wars-type things that look pretty violent to me."

Kerry didn't answer her for a moment, then he said thoughtfully, "The argument that is usually advanced is that toys, like books, mirror the society in which they flourish."

Nora thought he was making excuses for his company's products, but then he added firmly, "At Toys Unlimited we don't make war toys of any description. We believe violent toys promote violent behavior, and we want no part of it."

"Good for you," Lillian said.

"We do make a lot of stuffed animals," he added. "Not just for babies, but for the teenage crowd. Everyone needs something to cuddle." Another sly smile came Nora's way.

"I hope you don't use real animal skins," Lillian said as she piled dirty dishes on a tray. She was a sometimes embarrassingly vocal opponent of those who killed animals for their skins.

Kerry shook his head. "Never."

Lillian beamed at him.

"Actually," Kerry went on, obviously basking in her approval, "one of our fabric experts came up with a synthetic that looks and feels exactly like baby seal fur." He grinned reminiscently. "A very sexy lady, our fabrics expert. Greta Mallory."

Uh-huh, Nora thought.

"We're expecting big things from Greta," Kerry continued unabashedly. "A lot of fashion people are interested. I'm fairly fascinated by that area myself."

What area, Nora wondered.

Charlie and Lillian started carrying dishes into the kitchen, Charlie forestalling Nora's protest with a light "Stay and entertain your friend, dear," which brought her a wicked glance from Kerry. She had a pretty fair idea what kind of entertainment the remark had brought to his mind.

There was a short silence after Nora's parents had left the room, then Gregory said to Kerry, "I bet you play games all the time."

Nora waited for Kerry to deny it, but he didn't. "Only when I'm sure I can win," he said, looking directly at Nora.

This time even Gregory caught the double entendre. Nora saw him glance quickly from her to Kerry. His smooth forehead creased and he opened his mouth to say something, but then evidently thought better of it. Instead he said, "Kerry brought me a present, Mom. Can I show it to you?"

"May I," Nora corrected automatically, then glanced at Kerry as Gregory went clattering up the stairs to his room. "You shouldn't have, Kerry, it wasn't necessary."

"I wanted him to like me."

"You didn't think your delightful personality would be enough?"

"I believe in taking chances in some areas, but not all."

She frowned. "How did you find time to go shopping?"

There was something a little too innocent about his smile. "I didn't tell you we have a branch of Toys Unlimited in Oakland?"

"No." How many more surprises did he have in store for her, Nora wondered.

"Jordan and Bridget are joint managers," he told her. "As you may have gathered, they aren't always the most stable couple, so I have to keep an eye on them." He leaned forward across the table and covered her hands—clasped together on the raffia table mat—with his own, setting up an immediate warm clamoring within her.

"I think I may have to keep an even closer watch on the operation from now on," he said softly.

"No, Kerry," Nora objected, taking her hands away. "I don't think that's a good idea at all. I mean, it wasn't, I didn't . . . oh damn, I can't even talk straight."

"Then quit," Kerry suggested. "You aren't saying anything I want to hear, anyway."

"It was probably a mistake, Kerry," she said, trying again. "This weekend, I mean. We don't even know each other."

"Can you think of a more entertaining way to get acquainted?"

"Kerry. . ."

"This isn't the same as Kerry's plane," Gregory said, putting a long box on the table in front of her. "This is a sailplane . . . it won't need an engine. Isn't it neat?"

"You fly your own plane?" Nora asked, surprised.

Kerry nodded. "I often have to zip around from place to place. I flew here directly from Portland yesterday."

"Lots of businessmen do that, I guess," Nora murmured. "But somehow flying around in your own plane seems rather..."

"Frivolous?" His eyebrows were making fun of her.

"You've got to admit it does impart a certain reckless image," Nora pointed out.

He grinned. "I certainly hope so. If it doesn't I wasted a lot of money on that leather helmet and the goggles and the white silk scarf."

Gregory giggled. Nora sighed and looked down at the long narrow box her son had just opened. He was reverently handling sheets of balsa wood with wing-ribs stenciled on them, unfolding a blueprint. "We're going to cover the plans with wax paper so I can glue the pieces together right on top," he said excitedly.

"I don't know, Gregory," Nora murmured. "This looks a bit complicated, doesn't it?"

Gregory snorted in exasperation, and she looked apologetically at him. "I don't mean that it's beyond you theoretically," she explained. "But I'm not sure you're dexterous enough to cut out all these small pieces. You haven't done anything like this before. It must be pretty difficult."

"I'm going to help him," Kerry put in before Gregory could say anything. "I've never had a boy to play with," he added. "My sisters show a distressing tendency toward producing more of their own kind." He looked at Nora, saw that she was frowning, and added hurriedly to Gregory. "Why don't we go up to your room right now and pin the plans on that fiberboard your grandfather found for us? He also came up with a single-edged razor blade, so I can cut out enough pieces to keep you going until I get back."

"Until I get back," Nora echoed after the two of them had left the room. Obviously Kerry Ryan was planning another visit. Possibly several if he really intended helping Gregory build that plane.

That fact seemed to indicate it hadn't been a one-night stand after all. Evidently he wanted to pursue the relationship. But what did *she* want?

"I'm worried about Gregory," her father said, coming back into the dining area.

Alarmed, Nora looked up at him. "Why, what happened while I was gone?"

He shook his head. "Nothing happened, darling. I meant that I'm generally worried." He sighed. "I took him to the zoo last weekend, mainly to get him away from his telescope. We spent a long time in Gorilla World and he gave me this dissertation in simian behavior. That's what he called it, simian behavior, not 'the way apes act'. He said that their life-style is not exclusively arboreal. I had to look up arboreal in the dictionary when we got home. It means living in trees."

Nora smiled. "We watched a TV special about apes just before I left, Dad. That's how Gregory is, like a sponge soaking up information. It's not easy living with a kid who's so intellectually advanced, I'll grant you...he often makes me feel like a dumb bunny...but it's nothing to worry about."

"I didn't mean to imply there was something wrong with him," her father said. "I enjoy watching his mind work, you know that. What worries me is that his bril-

liance sets him apart from other kids. What other eight-
year-old is going to relate to a kid who talks about simian behavior, for crying out loud?" He frowned. "He
needs a father, Nora," he stated sternly. "I can take him
to ball games, but I'm not up to organizing a game of
football in the neighborhood, or coaching a Little
League team to encourage him to get involved with
other kids."

"I should think not, Dad," Nora said fondly. "You do
enough for him as it is. I agree that a father would be
helpful, but it's not that easy to find one, you know.
Most of the guys I've dated have started backing off the
minute they met Gregory. He's intellectually intimidating and—"

"Only to meatheads."

"Dad," she protested, then laughed. "Okay, so I
haven't always chosen my dates wisely."

"You serious about Kerry Ryan?" he asked. "I read
something between the lines when he was joshing you.
I'm not prying, believe me, but I saw the look on your
face a couple of times. You like that young man more
than a little. I can tell."

"Sure, I like him. As Kerry himself says, what's not
to like?" Actually, Kerry had asked what's not to love,
but she didn't want to use that word around her father
and give him more ideas than he already had. "How
could anyone be serious about Kerry?" she asked
lightly. "He's never serious himself."

"He's a nice guy all the same," Charlie said. "And he's
evidently a hard worker. I like the way he thinks about
things. *He* doesn't show any signs of being intimidated
by our young genius. He'd probably make a great fa-

ther. There's a childlike quality about him, not childish, I don't mean that, but a kind of happy-go-lucky quality that most of us lose when we grow up." He sighed. "Probably wouldn't do you any good to get serious about him, though. I've known a lot of men like him. Some of the younger guys on my crew... He's not about to be tied down, I'm afraid. And that's how he'd look at marriage—as a tying down."

"You were a bachelor for a long time yourself," she teased him, trying to cover up any feelings that might be showing on her face. "Yet all it took was one look at Mom and you laid your glorious freedom at her feet."

"I was younger than Kerry when I decided I was ready to settle down," he said. "It just took me another ten years to meet the right woman. But my mind was considering marriage all along. Is Kerry's?"

"I've just met the man, Dad," Nora protested.

"Time doesn't always make the difference."

"You may be right." She sighed. "No, Dad, his mind isn't set on marriage. It's set against it. He's definitely not the marrying kind."

"Discussed it, have you?"

"In a general way."

"Uh-huh." He leaned over to kiss her cheek. "I'm being a buttinsky. I worry about you."

"There's no need to worry," she said fondly. "Even if I don't ever find the right man, I'm perfectly capable of taking care of myself and Gregory. With a little help from a couple of wonderful people I know."

He grinned, then frowned. "Just so you don't get lonely," he said. "It's been a long time since I was lonely, but I remember the feeling. It's no fun at all."

Tell me something I don't know, Nora silently replied.

IT WAS HALF AN HOUR after her parents had returned to their own apartment before Kerry came down from Gregory's room. "I helped him get ready for bed," he told her. "We cut out quite a bit of the plane, and then spent a few minutes checking up on tonight's sky to make sure all the constellations were in their appointed locations. When his eyes started revolving like planets in orbit, I suggested he hit the sack."

"I'll go up and tuck him in," she said at once, getting to her feet.

"He's asleep already. But don't worry, I made sure he brushed his teeth."

Halfway to the door, Nora stopped and looked at him, unable to hide her disappointment. "I didn't even have a chance to talk to him."

He regarded her steadily. "You're telling me I shouldn't have come here?"

She sighed and returned to the sofa. "No, Kerry. It's just that I'm off-balance, I guess. I didn't expect . . . I'm not used to people who behave quite so unpredictably."

"Should I apologize?"

"No . . ." She hesitated, looking directly at him. "I think I like it."

Their eyes met and held. Conscious of tension, Nora laughed a little breathlessly and added, "It's good for Gregory to meet new people."

"What a mind he has," he enthused, sitting down next to her. "It's hard to believe he's not even nine years old yet. He told me he expects to become a scientist."

"He was taking watches and radios apart when he was five," Nora supplied. "He always wanted to find out how things worked. Most kids do, of course, the difference is that after asking where babies come from, Gregory went right on, without even pausing for breath, to ask where the universe came from. And he wasn't satisfied with any simplistic answer. He really wants to know. His counselor thinks he'll probably become a physicist."

"Raising such a prodigy is quite a responsibility for you, isn't it?" Kerry said thoughtfully.

"I look upon it as a privilege," she said, hoping he wouldn't find that statement pretentious.

He smiled warmly at her. "You would. You are a fine mother, Nora Courtney. Your son loves you a great deal. He went to great pains to tell me that you could have cooked just as good a dinner as Gran, and you wouldn't have forgotten the gravy. You may be a working mother, he says, but you can do everything stay-at-home mothers do too."

Nora laughed. "He always makes me sound like Supermom. He's the super one. He's so easy to get along with he's scary. Though we do have our problems, naturally."

Kerry nodded thoughtfully. "I found it interesting that he gave me a five-minute lecture on the movement of the stars and the rotation of the earth and had me look through the finder for Ursa Major and Ursa Minor, which I always knew as the Big and Little Dipper, but when I started to talk about the Indian legends about the bears that supposedly formed those constellations, he dismissed that as childish nonsense."

Nora sighed. "Yes, that about sums Gregory up. My father worries that he doesn't often act like a child. Which he doesn't. I sometimes think he was born old. And as long as he shoots ahead in school he's going to be behind his classmates in size and emotional maturity. At the rate he's going, he'll probably enter college when he's thirteen."

"I would think the most important thing is to accept him just the way he is. It would be easy to make him feel like a freak."

She was surprised by his insight. "Sometimes I manage to get him to remember he's a child," she said. "But I don't push it. Gregory is Gregory. As you commented, he's fine just as he is."

"He certainly is. I like him a lot. I'd like to help you with him, Nora."

She raised her eyebrows. "Without any ulterior motive in mind?"

He looked astonished. "My motives are always ulterior. Surely I haven't pretended otherwise?"

She laughed. "At least you're honest about it....I'm sorry, Kerry, I started to say earlier that I thought..."

She broke off. He had moved much closer to her and now he was touching her cheek, turning her face gently toward him. She couldn't remember what she had meant to say, or even what she had already said. Perhaps she ought to protest. "Kerry," she murmured, but it was too late. His mouth was already on hers, fitting it as though their lips had been cast from the same mold, and her own mouth was welcoming his kiss as though it had been starved for years. Her arms went up to pull him closer to her, and his arms slipped around her waist, his hands so warm, so gentle on the smooth silk of her blouse.

She thought to tell him she shouldn't do this—her parents might come back up, Gregory might wake—but the truth was Gregory always slept like a hibernating bear and her parents retired early on Sunday nights. Her father was an early riser, six o'clock on weekdays, and her mother, that happily unliberated woman, always got up to cook him a hot breakfast. No one and nothing would interrupt them here except traffic sounds and an occasional siren as a police car raced up and down hills, heading for some disaster or other.

He kissed her forehead, her cheeks and her mouth, again and again, then drew her head to his shoulder and stroked her hair, murmuring incoherently against her cheek.

They spent a long time kissing each other, discovering and establishing a rhythm that suited them both, brushing each others' lips, flirting with each others' tongues, laughing softly when their noses bumped, enjoying the newness that was not quite new.

It was over an hour before he even attempted to take her clothes off, and even then he took his time. First, he slowly undid the buttons of her lemon silk blouse one by one, making a teasing game of the suspense his slow movements were creating. His lips on her breasts moved her to tenderness as she touched his crisp light brown hair . . . there was something almost reverent in the delicate way he nursed at her breast. As though a cord joined breast to groin, she felt a tug of sensation every time his lips closed and opened, hardened and relaxed.

She sniffed deeply, appreciatively, in the hollow of his throat and pronounced the area deliciously fragrant, "Like thyme and rosemary when you crush them in your fingers."

He smiled lazily. "My sisters are forever poking bags of potpourri in my dresser drawers. Every once in a while they give me the wrong mixture and make my clothes smell like a flower garden. You wouldn't want to inhale around me then."

"Yes I would."

"You now," he said softly, "you smell like the color of your blouse, lemon and something else, verbena?"

"You have a good nose," she murmured, kissing it.

Some time later, she asked. "Aren't you ever going to take your tie off?"

He laughed without raising his head. He was trailing a slow line of kisses across one of her shoulders, eliciting starbursts in every pore. "I'm busy. Take care of it, will you?"

She did. Then she thoughtfully unbuttoned his shirt and removed that, and eased herself flat on the nubby white fabric of her cushioned sofa, pulling him down with her. He was still moving his hands very slowly over her, but she sensed a restraint in him now, as though he no longer wanted to take his time. He seemed reluctant to speed things up and thus propel the two of them toward the end of this time out of mind.

Out of mind. The thought echoed, but she refused to allow herself to dwell on any analysis of this situation. Every part of her body was feeling wonderful. Surely it couldn't be a mistake to let yourself feel wonderful.

She rotated her hips playfully under his. He raised himself with a hand on each side of her, and looked at her with narrowed eyes that hid all but a glint of green. "So, you want to get serious about this, do you?" he growled.

Instead of answering, holding his gaze with her own, she eased him to one side, then reached beneath herself to unfasten the zipper on her skirt. He responded by unzipping his denim pants, then matched her playfully move for move, kicking off his shoes as she let hers drop, wriggling out of his trousers as she eased out of her skirt, discarding his socks as she pulled down her panty hose, and finally, timing his motions exactly with hers, taking off his jockey shorts at the same moment that she parted with her lacy briefs.

Their bodies came together unencumbered, touching warmly from head to toe, smooth masculine flesh against even smoother, softer skin. As though some inner signal had been ignited in each of them, the rhythm they had established moved into a faster beat, echoing the hammering of Nora's pulses. Kerry rolled with her and lifted her on top of him, settling her down on him. The two of them were joined together in a thrusting, twisting, breathless dance of passion that eventually rolled them both down onto the cotton dhurrie rug and reversed their positions. And all the while they murmured to each other and kissed whatever part of the other's body presented itself and touched and caressed and stroked in intimate places, excitement growing in both of them, so that their breathing became ragged and rasping and their whispers became hoarse cries.

There came a time when Nora looked beyond the smooth tanned curve of Kerry's shoulder and focused on the plaster rosettes that festooned the edges of the ceiling. Her vision seemed extremely clear for a moment, and each plaster leaf and petal shone with crystal light. Her body arched with his, and they both hovered on the brink of that exquisite explosion that is unlike any other feeling in the world. Then, with one final thrust, he filled her entirely and she watched through a haze of heat as the rosette garlands danced and swirled and blurred and finally, inevitably, shattered.

5

ON FRIDAY, after cocktails in Nora's apartment and a discussion of her recent seminars, John Simpson Bradford treated Nora to dinner at his favorite restaurant, which was on the top floor of one of San Francisco's oldest and grandest hotels. He seemed unusually ill at ease while he ate, commenting several times on the magnificent view of the city as though he and Nora hadn't seen it dozens of times before, complimenting Nora extravagantly on her apricot silk dress as though he hadn't seen that before, either. He seemed to be avoiding her eyes, too, and John believed in eye contact as much as he believed in a strong handshake.

He *looked* okay, as well dressed as ever in a navy blue pinstriped suit, and a pale blue shirt that matched his eyes. His patterned red tie and pocket handkerchief were coordinated. His silver-gray hair, a perfect foil to his youthfully handsome face, had been impeccably blown into place by Ramon, the barber he always patronized.

There was a twitch beneath his right eye, Nora noticed as he talked jerkily about his week in Denver and the success of the regional office he had established there. But John was never nervous. Could it just be the light shining through his gold-rimmed glasses? No . . . there was a definite tic.

What on earth was wrong, she wondered as she toyed with her broiled fish and the superb chardonnay John had ordered. Was it something she had done? Her seminars in Alaska and Washington and Oregon had gone over extremely well. During the past week, while John was away, she had conducted another very successful two-day workshop in Los Angeles. And a mini-session yesterday afternoon at a bank on Montgomery Street. Had John somehow found out about her relationship with Kerry Ryan? She had an idea he'd disapprove of her getting involved with someone she'd met through a seminar.

She was being silly, she told herself. There was no way John could know about Kerry. She hadn't even seen Kerry since he left her apartment Sunday night, though he had sent her a comic greeting card every day. She bit her lower lip to hide a smile, remembering yesterday's offering—a man sympathetically holding an ice bag to his lady love's aching head. The card was captioned, "You are the sexiest thing I ever laid ice on."

"Is anything wrong?" John asked. "You were grimacing," he explained when she looked at him blankly.

"I was just thinking about something," she said hastily. "Actually, I was about to ask you the same question. You seem very nervous tonight."

"Do I? Yes, I suppose I must."

Not much of an explanation, she thought.

She finally found out what was on his mind after the extremely dignified headwaiter brought their dessert, a creamy concoction that must have contained several hundred calories. While Nora was slowly spooning it up, savoring every sinfully delicious mouthful, John suddenly placed his snowy napkin on the equally white tablecloth, leaned his elbows on the table and steepled his fingers. He was the only person Nora had ever seen do that in real life, though she had read of bankers doing it in novels. Was John going to offer her a loan?

Kerry Ryan's comic view of life had rubbed off on her, she decided. She must stop having such silly thoughts.

"I want to talk to you about something important, Nora," John said. His voice was so solemn that her stomach sank, effectively destroying the rest of her appetite.

Placing her spoon carefully in her dessert dish, she smiled tentatively at him. "That sounds very ominous, John."

He looked surprised. "Does it? I didn't intend it to. I just meant to sound serious and sincere."

That last word was an unfortunate choice. Nora was immediately reminded of Kerry Ryan saying of John's television appearances, "He looks so sincere and honest, like a politician, or a used car salesman."

"Did I say something amusing, Nora?" John asked.

She hastily straightened her expression. "I just remembered something," she murmured.

"You seem to be remembering several things tonight," he remarked. "It's not like you to be so distracted."

"I'm sorry, John. I'll try not to be so absentminded. What's the problem?"

"It isn't a *problem*, Nora," he corrected testily.

"I'm sorry," she said again. "You sounded so, well, so serious, I thought I must have done something wrong."

"You haven't done anything wrong, Nora," he said firmly. "You never do anything wrong. Nor do you ever let personal worries interfere with your professional duties, though I know you must have some."

"Not really, John," she said.

"Now, now, my dear, a woman alone...I know how resourceful you are, but surely it must get tough at times."

She wasn't at all sure what he was getting at, but in the hope of increasing her income, she murmured, "Well, it gets tight financially, but—"

"I *thought* I had seen that dress before," he said, nodding solemnly.

"You said you liked it."

"I do indeed." He frowned. "This conversation is getting off the track, Nora. I had no intention of criticizing your dress."

"Except to point out that it's getting too familiar? You know, John, I've seen that suit on you before too. Don't you think you're being a little chauvinistic? Why should women wear something different every time they appear in public? Men don't have to. They can go on wearing the same old corduroy jacket with leather patches on the sleeves, and everyone smiles fondly and says 'Oh, Joe does so love that old jacket of his.' But if a woman wears the same dress twice it's a whole other story." She knew she shouldn't tease him—Kerry's influence surfacing again—but all the same, the crack about her dress had been unfair.

"I meant only to show my concern for your problems as a single parent, my dear," John said soothingly. "I'm sure that it's very hard for you to give that miniature Einstein of yours all the attention he deserves when you have to travel so much and work such long hours."

She distractedly imagined what Kerry would say if he heard John calling Gregory a miniature Einstein. "Nora, I told you it was time to get that kid a haircut," he'd joke.

Was John going to fire her, she wondered abruptly. Was he calling her a neglectful mother? Had he decided he couldn't in good conscience contribute to Gregory's neglect? He had admired Gregory's mind, she knew, ever since Gregory had agreed with him that ESP hadn't been proven scientifically—which didn't mean Gregory didn't believe in it. John, on the other hand, didn't believe in anything he couldn't see or touch or hear. Again she heard Kerry's voice: *Not even electricity?*

"I have to work, John," she said, unable to hide her alarm. "Even if I didn't want to work, I need to work. Gregory's father has never contributed, and—"

"Nora," John interrupted. "I'm not expressing myself very well this evening, I'm afraid." He sounded surprised at himself, as perhaps he should be, considering he had made millions teaching others how to communicate effectively. "I didn't mean to sound critical of you, I just feel you shouldn't work quite so hard."

"I can't afford to go part-time, John."

"You could if—" He shook his head briskly. "Let's cut to the bottom line," he suggested. To her astonishment, he reached across the table, took hold of her hand between both of his and squeezed it, smiling encouragingly. Now what? He had never, ever, made the slightest suggestion of a pass. "In specific, behavioral, quantifiable terms," he began, "this is what I want. I want you to marry me."

The San Andreas fault, source of dozens of earth tremors every year, chose that moment to remind the residents of San Francisco that it was still there. The earthquake was minor, and the diners resumed their conversations after a few seconds of silent homage during which they watched the restaurant's spectacular chandeliers clatter and clink.

"I hope that was a good omen," John said with a twinkle in his eye, as unfazed as everyone else. In San Francisco, earthquakes were a fact of everyday life. Beyond the windows, none of the tall lighted buildings had developed a tendency to lean. All was well.

Nora must have gaped at John for a full minute after the earth stopped trembling, and still she didn't believe her own ears. It felt as though all the blood had left her face and pooled in her feet. The headwaiter had appeared at her side, his dignified face concerned above the starched expanse of his white shirt. "Some brandy perhaps, Mrs. Courtney," he murmured, obviously thinking she had been frightened by the earthquake.

She shook her head, and he backed away discreetly. Nora swallowed, and forced herself to look directly into John's benign, smiling eyes. "Well!" she said. Hardly a brilliant observation.

"I realize my proposal comes as a surprise to you," John said, empathizing in true John Simpson Bradford Seminar fashion. "Because of that I intend giving you plenty of time to think it over. Before you answer, I would like you to consider the benefits." He had used exactly the same phrasing when he offered her a job. "You mentioned finances. Gregory is going to require a great deal of money for his education. . . ."

"There are scholarships," Nora said faintly.

"Most scholarships won't begin to cover all the costs. Also, Nora, those costs are going to increase with inflation. If you were married to me he would never have to worry about money. He would be free to study, to experiment to his heart's content." He paused, as though to gather energy. The twitch was gone now and he was making strong eye contact, mesmerizing her with the intensity of his gaze. "You would benefit personally, too," he continued. "If you wished to stop working, I would be amenable to whatever domestic arrangements would suit you. If you preferred to carry on, then as my wife and partner you would spend your time here in the head office instead of out in the field. Your hours could be adjusted to meet your needs."

Oh, why had he tied in his proposal with a promise of a job in the head office? Head office was exactly what Nora wanted. She'd be close to home, near Gregory, available in the event of a crisis.

She couldn't marry John just so she could go home for lunch, of course. Or could she? She must at least hear him out, consider his proposal seriously. The trouble was that as John had shifted from the benefits to Gregory to the advantages for Nora, she had recognized section five of the seminar for middle-management supervisors. John was demonstrating *restructuring an idea so that it appeals to your listeners more and how to handle others' resistance to your ideas.* She kept wanting to giggle.

She tried to suppress all clues to her feelings, to allow herself to consider the arguments John was using... arguments that actually made a great deal of sense.

"You would have a free hand in redecorating my house... your furniture would fit right into the contemporary decor, wouldn't it? You will have a life free of financial worries...." John had switched to motivation through encouragement, using *positivetalk*, a concept he had developed.

He was thirty years older than she was. Had he thought of that? He was in great shape, of course. He jogged religiously five miles every day, though he had confessed to Nora that he didn't enjoy running because it seemed an inefficient use of time. Nevertheless, his skin was tight across his bones, his waistline trim. His hair was gray, but it was thick and healthy. She didn't love him—he could hold her hand all night and her heart wouldn't beat any faster—but she did admire him.

He was probably exactly the kind of man she ought to marry...solid, dependable, serious. Why, then, was she even thinking about the absence of love, meaning excitement, infatuation, stars in the eyes and a song in the heart. Hadn't she decided none of that constituted a sound basis for sharing your life with someone?

She was surprised, of course... she had certainly never imagined him proposing to her, even when Kerry asked if there was anything between them. All the same, there wasn't really any reason for her to feel quite so negative. What had happened to her desire for a stable, secure, settled life?

Kerry Ryan had happened. She had fallen in love with Kerry Ryan. Heaven help her.

She almost groaned aloud. Then she became aware that John had stopped talking and was looking at her expectantly. What on earth could she say? Certainly not any of the turn-of-the-century phrases that were floundering around in her mind: *Though deeply sensible of the honor... Unworthy as I am... Believe me, sir, I am cognizant of...*

"I don't know what to say, John," she said at last. "I'm really quite..." Her mind discarded shocked and flabbergasted and substituted overwhelmed, which was sufficiently ambiguous to make John smile hopefully.

"I knew you would be," he said confidently. "I'm rather overwhelmed myself. After the little woman passed on ten years ago, I knew I'd have to look around very carefully before I decided to remarry... Marian was so perfectly suited to my needs."

Nora suppressed a shudder. In her book, "little woman" was right up there with "hubby" and "better half." How had Marian's needs fared, she wondered. "Maybe you can never really replace her," she suggested.

"I don't expect to." He sighed, and finally let go of her hand. "I wouldn't look upon you as a replacement, Nora, believe me. You are very different from Marian, much more assertive, confident, decisive."

"All qualities we teach in John Simpson Bradford Seminars," she pointed out, hoping to lighten the atmosphere.

He beamed. "That we do."

"How would you benefit, John?" she asked with genuine curiosity.

"I'd have a beautiful woman in my home and office," he said promptly. "A ladylike young woman I could be proud of. Someone to share my ambitions and successes. Someone who understands what I'm talking about when I discuss my philosophies. Someone who believes in those philosophies. And also . . ." The experienced lecturer's expression left his face and was replaced by something gentler, fonder. Nora was sure he was finally going to express some interest in her personally, and she felt herself softening. She should have known he must really care.

"I've always wanted a son," he finished softly, "but I don't relate well to babies. Gregory is a fine boy, without the . . . frivolous aspects that affect most adolescents. I would be proud to be his stepfather, his patron."

It could very well be, Nora thought, somewhat put out, that Gregory was the main reason for this proposal. John was a proud man, he would enjoy being able to brag about his stepson's accomplishments. Probably, in short order, he wouldn't even refer to him as his stepson, but his son. That was quite a contrast to the way other men she'd dated felt about Gregory. They had seen him as competition for her attention.

"I guess I do need time to consider this, John," she said carefully. "I'd begun to think I'd probably stay single forever. I'm very flattered that you'd even consider me, but it may be that I'm too set in my ways."

"Nonsense," he said breezily with a wave of one impeccably manicured hand. "You're a flexible person, Nora. It's one of your qualities that I particularly admire. Ways, habits, mannerisms, all can be changed. That's another John Simpson Bradford maxim, remember?" He twinkled at her, and she suppressed another shudder at the thought of her preferences being dismissed so cavalierly. He smiled encouragingly at her. "Take all the time you need, my dear. Talk it over with your parents, with Gregory." He frowned. "As you know, I don't believe in dwelling on negative aspects of a situation, but I expect I should tell you that I'm not exactly, well, I'm not at all a passionate man. However," he added brightly, with a return of confidence, "I have an idea your own disposition is fairly. . . shall we say, cool?"

I can think of an Irishman with dancing eyes and a mustache and more than his fair share of muscles who would give you an argument on that, Nora thought, nettled by the suggestion that she might be frigid. However, it made no sense to argue the point, so she allowed a faint smile to signify agreement.

John beamed at her again, his gold-rimmed glasses shining in the light. "Now I have another surprise for you," he said. "You'll remember that I'm going to personally conduct a three-day seminar in Washington, D.C., the week after next?"

Nora nodded. "The White House employees. Quite a coup for you."

"To give us a chance to spend a little quality time with one another, I've decided to take you along with me, see how we do working together. How does that sound to you?"

"Fine," Nora said weakly. What else could she say? A horrible thought struck her out of the blue. When she turned John down, as she would have to turn him down, would he decide it would be uncomfortable for him to work with her? Would he fire her?

He was looking very pleased with himself. Probably he couldn't imagine her saying no. Probably he wasn't at all used to rejection. He might never have experienced it. She wondered if he would be able to handle it, what he would do.

He was rubbing his hands together now. She had never seen anyone else do that, either. "Now all that's out of the way," he said, signaling the headwaiter, "How about an after-dinner drink? Your usual crème de menthe?"

"I think I'll take that brandy now," Nora replied.

HER MOTHER was crocheting when Nora got home. Testing the waters, Nora told her of John's proposal, wondering what her reaction would be. She didn't have to wonder long. Lillian was of the opinion that Nora should have turned him down immediately. "He's nothing but a dirty old man," she said hotly as she gathered together the pieces of the afghan she was working on. "To think I've admired him. What a thing, to think he has a right to marry someone as young as you. I don't care how good it would be for Gregory. We can take care of Gregory ourselves. None of the frivolous aspects indeed."

After she'd left, still muttering, Nora noticed light on the attic stairs and went up to check on Gregory. He was lying flat on his back in bed, his hands clasped behind his head. He was staring up at the shadows the bedside lamp had flung on his ceiling, a worried expression on his thin freckled face. "What's up, sport?" Nora asked.

"Just thinking," he said.

"Don't give me that. Anytime you burn the midnight oil there's something weighty on your mind. What's going on?"

"Trouble at school," he said with a sigh.

"You? The original teacher's pet? What did you do, disprove somebody's equation? Question the laws of gravity?"

He shook his head. "We were talking about statistics and I said that the Golden Gate was one of the world's tallest and largest single-span suspension bridges with an overall length of eight thousand, nine hundred and eighty-one feet and that it was built at a cost of thirty-five million, five hundred thousand dollars."

"What's wrong with that?"

"Harvey Blassingame called me a know-it-all."

"Harvey Blassingame? Is he new?"

"He started after Easter. He's thirteen and almost six feet tall. A basketball jock and a computer whiz."

"King of the hill personified."

"Affirmative." That was Gregory's latest buzzword.

"So what did you do, challenge him to a duel?"

Her son regarded her in silence for a moment, his green eyes appraising, then he said, "Are you trying to get me to lighten up?"

"Something like that."

"It's not working."

"I'm sorry, honey, I've got things on my mind too. Tell me what happened. I'm listening."

"I told Harvey Blassingame I got the information off a picture postcard in Woolworth's, which anyone else could do unless his brain was the size of a pea."

"Ouch!"

"That's what I said when he hit me."

"He hit you? Where? Are you okay? Show me."

He didn't move. "There's nothing to show, Mom. He punched me in the chest and luckily I had my calculator in my inside jacket pocket." He grinned momentarily. "Sure surprised Harvey."

The shadows returned to his eyes. "After he finished rubbing his knuckles, he told me that was just a sample. That he was going to get me when nobody else was around. Then he called me a few nasty names."

"He sounds like a stereotype of a school bully."

"Except that he's a brain." He sighed. "I shouldn't have made the crack about his brain size. It isn't true."

He still sounded gloomy. Nora bent over him to kiss his forehead, and he pulled his arms out from behind his head and hugged her. "I'm not scared of Harvey," he said. "But he did make me mad. I don't like to be called names, especially by a jerk who . . ." His voice trailed away. "Am I really a wimp, Mom?"

"Harvey called you a wimp?"

He nodded. "A scrawny wimp," he said tightly, his voice sounding on the edge of tears. "Some of the other kids laughed."

She hugged him fiercely, then sat up and looked at him directly. "You are nothing of the sort. You are a good-looking healthy boy. You may be smaller than this jackass Harvey, but you're also five years younger. Your father was well-proportioned, your mother is well-proportioned, in all probability you will be too. In any case, you mustn't let negative thoughts about yourself enter your mind. No one can criticize you without your permission. If you don't allow your subconscious mind to take such thoughts literally, they can't affect your image of yourself."

His worried expression had disappeared as she talked. Now he gave her a humorously sly look that bordered on mischief. "You've been hanging out with John Simpson Bradford, haven't you?"

She grinned ruefully. "I was pontificating, huh?"

"Sort of."

She looked at him curiously. "What do you think of John, honey? Seriously?"

He considered for a moment, wrinkling his smooth forehead. "I like him, I guess. He never talks down to me. He treats me like a person. He's not a whole lot of fun, like Kerry Ryan, say, but he's okay. What he says makes sense, he just takes himself too seriously, so he comes off as dull."

"You constantly surprise me," Nora said.

"Is that good or bad?"

"Good. You have an amazing insight into people."

"Unless they're named Harvey Blassingame."

"You'll work it out, honey."

"Sure. I'll go with the flow."

Nora stood up and turned away. "I guess I'd better let you get your sleep," she said softly.

"You said you had things on your mind?" Gregory observed as he switched out his light. "Anything serious?"

What a sweetheart he was to remember.... She hesitated. "John asked me to marry him," she blurted out.

There was a silence. Then Gregory asked, "Did you say you would?"

"I told him I needed time to think it over." She sighed. "I didn't really need time, but I didn't want to insult him by saying no too fast. The trouble is, I need to come up with a good reason, or at least a tactful reason for saying no. I don't want to make him feel so uncomfortable that he'd decide he couldn't work with me."

"But you definitely don't want to marry him?"

"Absolutely not."

She heard his sigh of relief clear across the room. "I thought you said you liked him," she teased.

"I do. Dull is okay to visit once in a while. To live with is something else."

Nora laughed. Her son could always make her feel better. All the same, after she returned to the living room she sat in front of the empty fireplace for a while, wishing it were cold enough to light a fire. A fire would cheer her up. Incidents like the one with Harvey Blassingame worried her. She had an idea they might increase in direct proportion to Gregory's abilities. And she wasn't at all sure she knew how to handle them. She couldn't even handle her own problems.

If only she had someone to talk to....

What she really wanted, she admitted to herself after sitting and staring at the cold grate for an hour, was to have someone hold her and tell her everything was going to be all right. She had friends she could call, and either of her parents would be happy to come up and keep her company. But somehow a friendly or parental hug didn't seem to be what she needed.

Kerry Ryan's name kept coming to mind.

6

KERRY BOUNDED UP THE STEPS to the Courtney house, clutching The Stargazer, a stuffed comic tiger that was going to be Toys Unlimited's Christmas leader. The zany-looking animal had a pair of miniature binoculars around his neck and a star chart clutched in one paw. Other tigers in the line included The Doctor, The Fireman and The Teacher, all with their own special accessories.

In Kerry's other hand, he carried a bouquet of daisies he'd bought at a flower stand near Union Square; the daisies of course, had nothing to do with Toys Unlimited. It was two o'clock on a Saturday afternoon so it seemed possible that Nora would be home....

Gregory opened the door of the elder Courtneys apartment as Kerry entered the foyer. "I thought that was you," he exclaimed. "I saw you parking. How come you drove down instead of flying?" Worry lines appeared on his forehead. "Did you curb your wheels? This is a steep hill."

"I noticed," Kerry said. "And I drove down because I had more time this visit and sometimes I just like to drive. And yes, sir, officer, I did turn the wheels in—it's not my fault the stupid car rolled itself all the way down into the bay. Maybe it just wanted a bath."

Gregory grinned, taking at least twenty-five years off his face. "It's a neat car. What kind is it?"

"An old MG. Maybe you'd like a ride sometime. In the meantime, this fuzzy gentleman is for you." As he presented Gregory with the tiger, Kerry managed to keep his voice cheerful, although his usual high spirits had plummeted when Gregory opened the door. Because if Gregory was downstairs, then Nora probably wasn't home.

"He's great," Gregory exclaimed, sighting through the binoculars. "Hey, these really work. Thank you, Kerry."

"Nora's in Washington, D.C.," Lillian told him after searching out a vase for the flowers. "She and Mr. Bradford left on Thursday afternoon. They won't be back until Monday, I'm afraid."

"I didn't realize she and Bradford ever conducted seminars together," Kerry said as he accepted a cup of coffee.

"This trip is special," Gregory told him, seating himself on a nearby chair—cuddling the tiger, Kerry was pleased to see. "They've gone to the White House," he added in tones of awe, sounding for once like the eight-year-old he was.

"Nora's teaching the President how to shake hands?" Kerry asked, straightfaced.

Gregory exploded in little-boy laughter. "The seminar's for the White House employees," he explained. He frowned. "Mom wasn't expecting to go on this trip, but Mr. Bradford . . ." He hesitated, seemed about to say something more, but changed his mind and got very busy studying the tiger's goofy face.

"Problems?" Kerry asked.

Gregory shook his head, but he was still frowning fiercely. "I guess Mr. Bradford just wanted Mom with him," he finished lamely.

Kerry was as surprised by the shaft of jealousy that stabbed through him as he had been at the intensity with which he had missed Nora during the past three weeks—surprised and unnerved. He wasn't normally the jealous type. Love and let love was his motto, for others as well as himself. But Nora didn't seem to sit as lightly on his mind as other women had. In spite of the independent way she had about her, he had very quickly begun to feel protective toward her...and proprietary. That worried him in some vague way he didn't want to analyze.

She had insisted her relationship with John Simpson Bradford was strictly business when he joked about the man's sincerity, but all the same, Bradford was undoubtedly a handsome and charming man. Kerry's sister Colleen always claimed to suffer palpitations when he appeared on the television screen and looked straight into her eyes. The twins, Molly and Brenda, who always agreed on such matters, said he had that certain something Lee Iacocca had...an aura of power that was sexually stimulating. Even Bridget would roll her eyes and fan her face with one hand when he showed up on the screen.

"How come you're in San Francisco?" Gregory asked.

"It's rude to ask personal questions," his grandmother chided comfortably as she settled herself in an armless Victorian chair with a vividly colored, partially completed afghan and started plying a crochet needle.

"It's okay, Lillian, I don't mind," Kerry assured her. "I came to see how much progress you'd made on your airplane, Gregory."

"I bet," Gregory said with a snort, setting the tiger down on the floor. Kerry sensed a little hostility in his tone. Only total honesty would do for this boy.

"And at the same time to attend a strategy meeting at our Oakland plant," Kerry added smoothly.

"You didn't come to see my mother?" Gregory asked. "You brought those flowers for Gran and me?"

No fool he. Best to get the hostility out in the open. "Would it bother you if I did come to San Francisco only to see your mother?" Kerry turned to look the boy right in the eye.

Gregory hesitated, his green eyes fixed calculatingly on Kerry's face. "I'm having to make a lot of decisions about my mother's friends lately," he complained, a statement Kerry wasn't sure he understood.

After a moment that seemed to last forever, Gregory dropped his gaze and rubbed his nose hard, as though he were trying to erase his freckles. Then he picked up the tiger, sat it firmly on his lap, smiled shyly at Kerry and said, "No, I guess it wouldn't bother me."

"Me, neither," Lillian offered with a mischievously demure smile that made her look like her daughter.

Kerry grinned back, conscious of a warmth between the three of them that hadn't been there before. He had a feeling some kind of agreement had been reached, positions taken. There was a lot to be said for conspiracy, he decided.

"So when are we going upstairs to check on my airplane?" Gregory asked. "I'm a little worried about it. I think I understand in theory how it's all supposed to fit together, in practice I'm pretty sloppy with the glue."

He hadn't exaggerated, Kerry discovered. The fiberboard on his desk looked as though a chorus line of snails had high-kicked across it, leaving thin white trails behind them. Lumps of glue had hardened on the edges of several wing ribs. All the same, for an eight-year-old he had done a creditable job of putting the wing together, and Kerry was able to offer genuine praise.

Gregory positioned the tiger on the stool he used with his telescope in his attic bedroom "So he can keep an eye on things," he joked.

He and Kerry worked happily together for a while, Kerry cutting out pieces of fuselage, Gregory sanding them lightly, until Kerry suggested they go out. "I'll have to get permission from your grandmother," he cautioned, "but I'm sure she won't mind."

"We could go to the Exploratorium in the Palace of Fine Arts," Gregory suggested. "It's not like a regular science museum, they don't have a bunch of annoying rules." He glanced at his wristwatch and sighed. "It closes at five, though, so we wouldn't have much time."

"It's also indoors. Don't you think we should take advantage of the sunshine?"

Gregory sighed again. "Don't you start on me, Kerry. Mom and my grandparents are always trying to get me outside. Grandpa is fishing for stripers today. He tried to talk me into going with him, but I knew he'd have a better time with his friends if he didn't have to worry about whether I was having a good time. I'm not so sure with all the cars around that the fresh air everyone's always raving about is so fresh anyway." He wrinkled his nose. "I've nothing against the outdoors, you know, it's just that most of the things I like to do are indoors. My grandfather worries that I'm not enough of a kid."

"Well, I'm enough of a kid for both of us. And I'm already disappointed because your mother isn't home, so as my host you have an obligation to cheer me up. And I *love* the outdoors."

Gregory sighed audibly, humoring him. "Okay, okay. What do you want to do?"

"Fly a kite?" Kerry suggested on the spur of the moment.

"That's kid stuff."

"Benjamin Franklin didn't think so."

Gregory looked at him approvingly. "You mean his famous kite-flying experiment where he proved that the atmospheric electricity that causes thunder and lightning is exactly the same as the electrostatic charge on a Leyden jar?"

It wasn't Kerry's first experience of Gregory's intellectual precocity, but it was the most astonishing so far. Somehow he managed to nod as though the boy hadn't said anything unusual. "That's the one. What do you say? If it's good enough for Franklin, it ought to be good enough for us. Who knows, maybe we'll discover something."

They bought a brilliantly colored, forty-five-foot dragon kite in Ghirardelli Square, then drove up to Twin Peaks to fly it. There was just enough breeze to make kite-flying easy, and enough gusts to take the predictability out of it. "I can never get a kite as high as

I want to," Gregory complained. "Even though I've worked out the right kind of string to use."

"How do you do that?" Kerry asked.

"You measure the total area of the kite and multiply by three, and that gives you the right line strength," Gregory said matter-of-factly, as though it was something every eight-year-old knew.

Kerry shook his head, impressed again. "I'll have to remember that," he said. "As for getting the kite up high, you have to let it know you're in control. Pulling it in causes it to gain altitude because you're pulling it against an air current," he added, demonstrating.

"Makes sense." Gregory nodded solemnly.

"The trick is to pull it in with a jerking motion, hand over hand, like this, then let it loose so it drifts outward with the wind. This way. Give and take," Kerry concluded, handing the spool over to the boy.

"You sure know a lot about kite-flying," Gregory said, trying out Kerry's suggestions with immediate success.

"I've spent a lot of time at our lodge on the beach in Oregon," Kerry told him. "My nieces often fly kites there." He glanced down at the boy, who was frowning in concentration as he handled the line. "You should come visit."

"I'm not much of a beach person."

"I was thinking more of your telescope. You were complaining last time I was here that there's too much light pollution from the city for you to see the night sky clearly. At my lodge it's totally dark. Not even a street-light. And there's a sort of widow's walk around the attics. You'd get an uninterrupted view of the sky from there."

"It's totally dark?" Gregory gazed eagerly up at him. He had apparently forgotten all about the kite. Kerry had to move fast to grab the string as he let go of it.

I've got him, Kerry decided, as Gregory apologized and took hold of the line again. If he invited Nora to the lodge in Gregory's presence, Gregory would probably help persuade her to accept the invitation.

Maybe, he decided, it would be best not to think about why he wanted so badly to spend as much time as possible with Nora Courtney.

They flew the kite for forty-five minutes, "the highest-flying kite in the world," Gregory proclaimed.

For once he didn't look as though the weight of the world was on his shoulders. With his dark brown hair blown around by the wind, his slightly oversized ears tinged with pink, his freckles darkening in the wind, he looked like any other eight-year-old in a yellow windbreaker and blue jeans and Nikes.

"I do believe you are having a good time," Kerry teased him.

Gregory nodded. "I am." As though belying his words, he tugged at his bangs and furrowed his brow, which made him look years older again. If this kid didn't watch out he was going to develop wrinkles before he was twenty, Kerry decided.

"You sure?"

Gregory nodded again, more briskly. "This was a good idea, Kerry. I'm glad you talked me into it. It took my mind off my troubles."

"What troubles?"

"Nothing you'd want to know about."

Kerry eyed him sideways. Gregory was trying to sound unconcerned, but Kerry knew he wouldn't have brought up the subject if he hadn't wanted to talk about it. "Try me," he suggested lightly.

Pulling in the kite, Gregory frowned in apparent concentration at the spool as he wound the string on it. "There's this guy who's giving me a hard time at school. Harvey Blassingame."

"You aren't on vacation yet?"

"Our school doesn't take long holidays like a regular school. We have too much work to do. Schools in other countries don't close down all summer, either. It's not really necessary, you know," he added in the amusingly pedantic manner that made him seem so much older than he really was. "We'll get August off, which is more than enough." He wrinkled his brow as though trying to recall what he'd been talking about.

"Harvey Blassingame," Kerry prompted.

Gregory sighed. "Harvey says I'm a know-it-all. He's a lot bigger than me so I have to pay attention to his opinion, though the school we go to is *for* know-it-alls."

He'd inherited his mother's wry sense of humor, but it was just barely showing through. "He wants to push me around, twist an arm or a leg here and there," he went on. "I'm not much of a fighter. It doesn't make sense for me to fight back anyway. Harvey could grind me into sausage meat with one hand tied behind his back."

"I don't believe in fighting, either," Kerry agreed. He considered a moment, then said, "So if you don't want to fight, you have to somehow disarm the enemy, right? Maybe you should try bribery."

"I'm serious, Kerry."

"So am I." Kerry helped Gregory fold the kite's tail over and over its body. Together they put the neat bundle into the "Come Fly A Kite" bag, then hiked back to Kerry's car and deposited it in the back.

They stood in silence for a few minutes beside the small red car, looking down to where Market Street slashed like a broadsword toward the tall buildings downtown and on to where sailboats dotted the calm bay. The breeze was blowing fresh and clean from the sea. Everything below them seemed to be sparkling.

"Isn't bribery illegal or immoral or something?" Gregory asked.

"Not if it's handled properly," Kerry answered him. "I'm not talking about money bribery, you know, I'm talking about doing something nice for him, giving him a present, a treat, being so nice to him that he can't find any reason to hate you so he has to start being nice to you."

There went the forehead again, wrinkling up like corrugated cardboard. Kerry reached out and tapped the lines. "Relax."

Gregory smiled vaguely. "My mother's always doing that," he said. "She keeps telling me wrinkling my forehead doesn't really help me to think more clearly, it just seems that way."

"She's right. I always prod my thinking processes this way. Much more practical."

He tugged at one end of his mustache to demonstrate, and Gregory laughed. "I guess I'll have to grow one. But it might take a while." He was silent for a moment, then with an air of astonishment said, "You know, your idea isn't bad. It just might work."

Kerry grinned. "Sure it'll work. It's even in the Bible. It's called loving your enemy. Enemies find it a very confusing approach. Harvey may even learn to love you back."

Gregory made a face. "I'm not sure I want Harvey Blassingame to love me, but I'll sure give your method a try." In spite of his attempted cynicism, he sounded relieved.

A few minutes later, Kerry suggested they go in search of dinner. They got back in the car and went on their way, Gregory complimenting Kerry on his driving ability. "Some people are scared of driving in San Francisco," he commented, "but you take your foot off the accelerator at just the right moment before going over a hill, so you don't shoot over the top, or stall and roll back."

Kerry felt absurdly pleased at this flattery. Gregory's opinion was beginning to matter to him, and not just because he was romancing the boy's mother.

"SO I'VE THOUGHT it all through, and it seems to me that you ought to marry Kerry Ryan," Gregory said calmly.

He had been sitting on the window seat, clutching the ridiculous tiger Kerry had given him and singing Kerry's praises ever since Nora arrived home an hour ago. Evidently Kerry had suggested a course of action with Harvey Blassingame that Gregory had put into motion this morning with some success. "Harvey's really confused," he'd gloated.

Unlocking her garment bag, which Gregory had helped her lay out on her low platform bed, Nora pulled the hangers free and took her dresses and extra suit to her mirror-fronted closet. "What makes you think Kerry's marriage material?" she asked. "The fact that he knows how to fly a kite?"

"The fact that he's *nice*," Gregory said, ignoring her levity. "He likes me and I like him. We get along great. After we flew the kite, he took me to Bobby Rubino's Place For Ribs at the Wharf because they have a kids' menu. He *knew* they had a kids' menu. And we talked about a whole lot of things . . . the ocean and the tides and the moon and what a long time it takes to grow up and how tough life is for American farmers and how awful things are in Africa right now . . . and toy-making. Did you know that chess started in India five thousand years ago?"

"I'll grant you that Kerry's interesting . . . and nice," Nora said, sorting through panty hose and briefs. "And I'm glad you like him. But fascinating conversation isn't all marriage is about."

"You could tell Mr. Bradford you couldn't marry him because you were going to marry Kerry. Then his feelings wouldn't be hurt."

Nora ruffled his hair and aimed a mock punch at the tiger as she went past the two of them with a couple of blouses. Precocious her son might be, but he had a lot to learn in some areas.

"Don't you like Kerry?" he persisted. "He likes you. He brought you flowers on Saturday and he sends you a card every day so that your memory will keep him evergreen."

The facetious phrase, obviously a quote, sounded so much like Kerry, brought him so much to life in her mind, that Nora felt a tug at her heart. "He's a character, isn't he?" she remarked carefully. She glanced at her son, who was gazing hopefully up at her. "I like Kerry, yes," she admitted.

"Well, then, why don't you want to marry him?"

He had put the tiger's arms—or were they paws?—around his neck, and was gazing into its bulbous eyes. There was a bleak look on his face suddenly. His voice, Nora realized, had lost the eagerness it had started out with.

Folding the garment bag and setting it on the floor, Nora sat down on the window seat and put an arm around her son. "You're serious about this, aren't you?"

He nodded, still looking at the tiger. "I felt so good when I was with Kerry. Driving and going out to eat. Like we belonged together. Like I was a normal kid and he was my dad."

Nora swallowed. "You are perfectly normal. But Kerry's not your dad, Gregory. He went right back to Oregon on Saturday night, didn't he?"

"I don't know, he didn't say. He was down here for some kind of meeting."

"Whatever. He may turn up in another month or he may not. You've liked guys that I've gone out with before, remember, then you get upset when they disappear. Remember last year? Bruce somebody, the man who always wanted to take me dancing?"

"Bruce Morgan." Gregory never forgot a name.

"You thought you'd like him to be your father because he knew what a catadioptric telescope was."

"I was just a kid then."

"I see. And now you're a mature adult and know what's best for me."

He looked sideways at her. "Are you mad at me?"

"Of course not."

"You sound mad."

"I'm not mad, Gregory. I'm just feeling tired and irritable generally. It was a stressful seminar." An understatement. John was becoming a problem. He had taken to looking at her soulfully, sighing once in a while, asking her every day, "Have you had a chance to think about my proposal?" So much for his promise to give her time. She felt as though every nerve in her body was coiled like a watch spring.

How could she tell Gregory that she was also irritated by his ridiculous championing of Kerry Ryan, mostly because she hadn't been able to get the damn man out of her mind while she was gone? "Look, honey," she said, hugging him close, "Kerry's a lot of fun and we can enjoy him as a friend, but he's not the marrying kind, so don't go getting your hopes up, okay?"

"Don't you ever want to get married?"

"Sure I do, if I can find someone decent and honorable and kind who also wants to marry me and is younger than John Simpson Bradford. Don't hold your breath. Anyway, let's face it, sport, every time I've gotten involved with anyone so far we've had problems, right?"

"Right," Gregory said with feeling.

"The guy always resented the time I spent with you, or else didn't want you to join us when we went somewhere. So as long as you and I are getting along okay maybe we don't need a third person in the act. Right?"

"Right," Gregory repeated, but he didn't sound quite so convinced this time.

About to launch into a more in-depth explanation, Nora gained a reprieve when the doorbell rang. That was probably her mother, wanting to hear all about the nation's capital.

Gregory ran off to answer the door and Nora started emptying her tote bag onto the bed. A moment later, she crossed the room to open a window. The day had turned into one of San Francisco's rare hot ones, with temperatures in the eighties. As the climate was usually temperate, her father hadn't included air conditioning in his remodeling plans. The sea breeze was usually enough to cool the place down, but unfortunately the open window also let in all the sounds of the city, which could sometimes be deafening. Because of this, it was a minute or two before Nora realized that Gregory sounded far more animated than he usually did when he greeted his grandmother. He was laughing riotously at something. And now she could hear another sound, an unfamiliar yipping noise that sounded suspiciously like a windup toy of some kind.

A toy?

Kerry's voice said, "My meeting finally let out. . . ."

Trying not to notice that her heart had jumped as though afflicted with hiccups, Nora forced herself to move slowly across the bedroom and down the narrow hall to the apartment's foyer. Smoothing her skirt and her hair into place as she went, she hoped her cheeks didn't look as flushed with heat as they felt.

Kerry was leaning in the front doorway, grinning down at Gregory, who was crouched over something on the floor. He had dressed for the hot weather in the green knit shirt and denim cutoffs he'd worn when she first met him. But it wasn't déjà vu that made her heart bump against her ribs a second time.

The moment he caught sight of her, Kerry straightened and smiled. He looked at her very directly, as though trying to memorize every detail of her tangerine blouse and oatmeal skirt.

She looked drawn, he thought, as lovely as ever but tired, tense around the edges, maybe worried about something. She was gazing silently at him, her wonderful brown eyes fixed on his face. He couldn't tell if she was pleased to see him or irritated that he had dropped in unannounced again. "Hi," he said brightly. "How was the White House?"

"Interesting. Intimidating."

Nora could feel a number of her nerve ends uncurling as she looked at him. Her fatigue and irritation seemed to be fading away. "How are you, Kerry?" she said. Of its own accord, her voice seemed to caress his name.

Then the toy he'd brought Gregory yipped again and she looked down, startled, to see that it wasn't a toy after all. It was an Irish setter pup whose ears and feet had grown at a faster rate than the rest of him. When Gregory released him, he bounded clumsily toward Nora, but skidded to a stop before he reached her, plopped back on his haunches and made the yipping sound that had first attracted her attention.

"His name is Rusty," Gregory said excitedly. "Isn't he terrific?"

"He's a darling," Nora said, crouching down and extending a hand to the pup. The dog sniffed her hand perfunctorily, then gave it a wet once-over with a surprisingly long pink tongue. Nora laughed and glanced up at Kerry. "I remember you mentioned an Irish setter. I take it this is part of a new generation."

"One of four. The pick of the litter."

The phrase aroused her suspicions. Standing, she looked Kerry in the eye. "It was thoughtful of you to bring him to visit us," she said, with a strong emphasis on the last couple of words.

He immediately looked sheepish, confirming her suspicions. "Kerry, you didn't!"

"Rusty's not visiting," Gregory informed her gleefully. "Kerry brought him for me to keep. Isn't he super?"

She wasn't sure if he was referring to the dog or the man, but it didn't make much difference. "No," she said, but Gregory wasn't listening. Lifting the little dog into his arms, he turned a radiant face to Nora, then headed out the front door. "I've got to show Rusty to Gran and Grandpa," he shouted over his shoulder as he shot off down the stairs.

"I can't believe you could be so irresponsible, Kerry," Nora exclaimed. "How could you bring Gregory a dog without even consulting me? It isn't fair to the puppy or to Gregory. Not to mention my folks. It's bad enough I have to rely on them to take care of my son when I'm not here. I certainly can't expect them to care for a dog too. They aren't young people. They like things quiet.

And he's not even a small dog. I mean, he is now, but he won't be. Irish setters get pretty big. They need a house and a yard to roam in. An apartment is no place for a dog at all, never mind a big dog. You could at least have brought the idea up first before saying anything to Gregory. Now you've got him all excited, and I'm going to have to break his heart. How do you think I feel about that?"

He had stopped looking sheepish and was gazing at her admiringly, which infuriated her. "Don't you dare tell me I look beautiful when I'm angry," she said through clenched teeth. "Your blarney isn't going to work this time, Kerry Ryan."

"But you do look beautiful, Nora darling," he protested. "Though I wasn't going to say so. I knew that would inflame you even more. What I was going to say is that you really do know how to be assertive. Comes of studying John Simpson Bradford's words of wisdom, I've no doubt. I'm sorry I missed half your seminar. I might have learned how to be assertive back."

"It wouldn't do you any good," she said firmly. "I'm sure you can see that you've made a mistake. You can tell Gregory so. I see no reason for me to be the ogre in this."

"But it isn't a mistake, Nora darling," he said softly. Reaching behind him, he pushed the door closed, then took her elbow, turned her around and eased her into the living room. "Let's sit down and talk this over like a couple of reasonable adults," he suggested, pulling her down beside him on the sofa.

"There's only one reasonable adult here," she pointed out. "The other one's taken leave of his senses. Don't you think I have enough problems . . ."

"Hush now," he said, touching her lips with a gentle thumb. Even through her anger she felt the shot of adrenaline that went through her at his touch, but she steeled herself against it.

"Something that lights up a boy's face like that can't possibly be a mistake," Kerry said.

"You could at least have asked me first."

"You'd have said no."

"Of course I would."

"That's why I didn't ask you. I wanted you to see what a dog could do for your son first. Did you ever see him look so much like a little boy?"

"That's not the point. . . ."

"It's very much the point. That's a very *happy* little boy. And the dog can only go on giving him happiness. Rusty will love him without question. He'll always be there for him. Something for him to cuddle, to confide in. I'm not sure it's even possible for a boy to grow into a man without a dog. I never could have made it without mine to talk to."

"I'm not sure you have made it." She sighed. "My father's going to be very upset, Kerry."

"On the contrary, your father thinks it's a grand idea. He'd thought of it himself, but he didn't think you'd want a dog up here with all your white furnishings. And if he kept a dog downstairs Gregory would be wanting to spend all his time down there, which might have led to problems between you, so he didn't suggest it. I assured him I could talk you around."

"Did you now? And when did you have this big discussion with my father? Just now? After you'd already brought the dog here?"

"No, I would never take an animal to a place where it might not be welcome. I talked it over with Charlie and Lillian on Saturday after I brought Gregory back." He was looking impossibly virtuous. "They agreed with me that having a dog would get Gregory out of the house more. He'll have to walk Rusty every day. That will also teach him responsibility." Obviously sensing that she was weakening, he wrapped his arms around her, pulled her close and brushed his lips across her forehead, tickling her with his mustache.

She giggled and he leaned back to look at her approvingly. "I knew you'd see the sense of it when you had a chance to think. You can't bring yourself to break that poor little boy's heart, can you? You won't be sorry. Rusty's a well-behaved little beast. He hardly ever misses his newspaper...."

"Hardly ever?"

"And he's been taught not to jump on the furniture. The thing about a big dog, you see, is that as long as you train him early then he isn't likely to climb around on top of things as a small dog would. You've got to admit, Nora, that he's a bit of a charmer."

She sighed. "I suppose he is."

"And if it didn't work out, you could always return him to me."

"I could?" His face was very close to hers again, and it was difficult for her even to remember what they had been arguing about.

"Am I forgiven for my sins?" Kerry asked several hours later. They were sitting together on the sofa again. Somehow Nora had been talked into allowing Rusty to stay.

"I've been thinking of inviting you both to the lodge for the Fourth of July weekend," Kerry had said over dinner. "Why not see how Rusty does until then? If it's not working out you could bring him back with you."

Fully intending to turn down the invitation while accepting the idea of returning Rusty, Nora had been outmaneuvered again. "I could bring my telescope," Gregory had exclaimed. "It gets dark there, Mom. Kerry says it gets really dark."

"Your mom knows that," Kerry had informed him. "She even got lost in the bathroom."

Luckily, Gregory was so excited about the prospect of visiting Kerry's lodge he hadn't thought to question Nora about that particular incident. His eyes had shone as brightly as the stars he was planning to watch. Looking at his eager face, how could she say no to the invitation? How could she say no to the dog?

Her consent had prompted a lot of activity. Gregory and Kerry had gone dashing off to City Hall to buy a license. They had also brought back dog food, a collar and leash, and a round padded bed. After dinner, Kerry and Gregory had put in some quiet work on the model airplane's stabilizer, so Rusty could have a chance to settle down, as Kerry had put it.

He had gone on to tell Gregory that he belonged to a model-airplane club in town and went to the meetings as often as he could. "You can join, too, once this plane is finished," he'd told him, then glanced at Nora.

"The members range in age from six to seventy and come from all walks of life," he'd told her. "Nothing like a common interest to break down societal barriers."

Obviously he'd conceived the model airplane project in order to help round out Gregory's social life. Just as obviously, he was anxious to assure Nora that Gregory would not feel out of place at the club meetings, that distinctions would not be drawn because of intellectual differences. Looking into his unusually solemn eyes, Nora had felt her heart contract with love for him.

Now both dog and boy were sound asleep in the attic, Gregory's crazy-looking tiger tucked in beside him. The last time Nora had peeked into the room, she could have sworn all three were smiling.

"You're forgiven," she told Kerry. "Only because I'm too tired to argue anymore."

"You look tired," he said sympathetically. "I thought that the minute I saw you."

"Flatterer," she murmured.

"Is anything wrong?" he asked. "Gregory indicated there might be a problem with John Simpson Bradford." It was a shot in the dark but he'd obviously hit the bull's-eye.

"What did he tell you?" she demanded, sitting up very straight. "I'll skin him alive. He knows he's not supposed to discuss family business—"

Kerry's fingers touched her lips, silencing her, then cupped her cheek, which had become extremely pink. "I asked Gregory how come you went on a seminar with John Simpson," he explained. "He hesitated and frowned and I asked if there was a problem and he shook his head. Pretty discreet behavior for an eight-year-old, I'd say."

"Oh."

"But there is a problem, isn't there?"

She sighed. "John asked me to marry him."

Kerry didn't usually suffer from indigestion. Earlier, he and Nora had cooked up some excellent Ohm rice in her wok. Surely there wasn't anything in rice and vegetables in an omelette envelope to give him this sudden searing heartburn?

"Aren't you going to say anything?" Nora asked.

He forced a grin. "What's to say? You obviously aren't dancing with glee, so I'd hazard a guess that you aren't about to become Mrs. John Simpson. You told him no, I take it?"

"I haven't told him anything so far."

"Why not? You couldn't possibly be in love with him."

"I respect and admire him."

He shook his head. "You can't get married unless your heart bounces around in your chest when you look at the man."

Nora laughed. "Listen to the expert on marriage."

"I've given a lot of sisters away, remember. All their hearts were bouncing. So why haven't you told John to buzz off?"

"I'm afraid he might decide to fire me if I turn him down."

"This from the woman who accused me of sexual harassment over one kiss? If he fires you, take him to court. There are laws."

"That's all very well, but think how uncomfortable it would be to work for him once I tell him no. I'd probably have to resign."

"So come to work for me. I have a vacancy in the marketing department."

She looked startled. "You'd really give me a job? Just like that?"

"Without any references. Though I'd reserve the right to chase you around your desk every day at high noon."

She made a face at him, then kissed him softly on the lips. "Thank you, Kerry. In spite of the rider I appreciate the offer, especially as you made it without hesitating. But I was hopeless at advertising, remember? I'd be even worse in any kind of sales. Besides, I love my work. And of course I'd never leave San Francisco."

He studied her alertly. His indigestion had taken a sudden turn for the worse. "Never?" he queried.

"My roots are here, Kerry. Roots are important to me. Aren't they to you?"

He shook his head. "I guess not. Not as they relate to a physical place anyway. No one place is particularly important to me. I can be happy anywhere. As long as I can see my family regularly." He frowned at her. "You'd never leave San Francisco?" he repeated. His indigestion wasn't going away.

Nora looked at him curiously, evidently noticing that he wasn't feeling too lively. "Well, obviously, I do leave it from time to time," she said patiently. "I meant I wouldn't want to live anywhere else. I love this city, Kerry."

He nodded, looking at her thoughtfully. "I can understand that." He raised an eyebrow. "Is John Simpson Bradford a native son?"

"Born and bred." She raised her eyebrows. "Maybe I haven't made this clear. I don't want to marry John." This firm statement had the effect of curing his indigestion immediately. A miracle.

"But you don't want to risk losing him either," he suggested.

"Not if it means losing my job."

"So what are you going to do?"

"I wish I knew. I'll just let some time go by, I guess." She chuckled. "He kept telling me what benefits I could expect, as though the whole thing was an insurance proposal." She sighed, sobering abruptly. "He also promised me time to think it over, but he's not being as patient as I expected. All the same, I think I can probably put off answering him at all for a month or so. Maybe I'll have a brilliant idea in the meantime."

"Or maybe I will."

"Be sure to share it with me."

He hugged her. "We're friends again, aren't we? I'm glad you decided to forgive me for introducing Rusty into the family."

"I'm not sure I should have forgiven you that easily," she said with a sigh. "Heaven knows what you'll come up with next."

"Well, as a matter of fact, I do have an idea of how we might spend the next hour or so."

"I bet you do."

He must have perfected the virtuous expression with constant practice. "You're misjudging me again, Nora. What I have in mind is for us to play a game."

She looked at him blankly. "A game."

"A new board game we're developing at Toys Unlimited. I thought you and I could test it out." He stood up. "Shall I run down and get it out of the car?"

"You really did bring a game?"

He shrugged apologetically. "It's a bit rough yet, but yes, it's a game."

She shook her head when he set off down the stairs. As she had told him before, he was not the most predictable of men.

A few minutes later she wasn't so sure about that. Kerry laid out on her sheet glass coffee table a board marked with a complicated grid whose destination was a central circle featuring a man and woman in a clinch, two sets of question cards with varying scores for different answers, and two plastic markers shaped like a man and a woman.

"The game is called Matchmaker," Kerry told her with a teasing glint in his eye. "You gave me the idea with all your talk about serious relationships. It's designed to help a man and woman decide how compatible they are. Terrific social value, don't you think? No more do men and women have to depend on burrs sticking to their sweaters. Now they can be sensible pragmatists instead of irresponsible sexual adventurers. After playing this game they can travel the road to destiny secure in the knowledge that they share goals and ideals and interests."

"Any game like that is going to prove that we shouldn't have anything to do with each other," Nora suggested slyly.

"Don't worry. If that happens, I'll rewrite the rules. You go first, okay? Pick a card."

"Are you serious?" Nora demanded, scanning some of the cards. "'Does he fool around with other women?'" she read aloud. "'If so, make him take five paces backwards. Does he scratch himself in public? Ten paces backwards.'"

"It's the small irritations that ruin a relationship," Kerry murmured.

One hilarious hour later, they had each confessed that they hated even the idea of anyone blowing in their ears. She had learned that he snored when overtired, that he put on his left shoe before his right though he always wanted to put the right one on first. "I don't believe in conforming even to my own brain's rules," he'd told her.

He had also confided that he loved liver and onions but not necessarily together, and that he always wet his toothbrush *before* putting on the toothpaste.

He had learned that she hated getting up in the dark, loathed the smell of onions, and never bought anything that needed to be ironed.

"You're very negative, Nora, did you realize that?"

He picked another card before she could answer. "'Do you like the way she kisses?'" he read aloud. "'Spend fifteen minutes finding out.'"

"Oh, I do like that one," he said, and proceeded to demonstrate. As usual, the moment he took her in his arms, Nora's senses disintegrated. First her heartbeat escalated, then her body pressed itself closer to him, and she noted that the knit fabric of his green shirt felt soft and smooth under her hands. It was only a short distance from that thought to the one about how smooth the skin under that shirt had felt the last time they were naked together.

She thought about that for quite a while as she kissed him just as thoroughly as he was kissing her. She kissed him slow and deep, her breath surging forward to meet his, her tongue delicately flirting with his, her upper lip receiving the sensuous brush of his mustache. Then, somehow, his shirt was off and so was hers. She was swaying against him on the sofa, feeling like a tree about to fall. The game was forgotten. They shed the rest of their clothes quickly, efficiently, and then his hands moved slowly, silkily over her breasts. She shivered with pleasure.

Then they were both kissing everywhere, shoulders, nipples, his chest, her breasts, his tightly muscled abdomen. And not only kissing but licking, nibbling, exploring each other with delight...open, free, touching everywhere, looking at each other, seeing no defects, though of course there were defects, everyone had defects.

He was growing hard. She could feel him swelling against her, and she wanted him inside her. As though the wish had to be granted immediately even though it hadn't been expressed, he lifted himself over her and a moment later they were moving in rhythm, speeding, slowing, speeding again. One of them—Nora wasn't sure which—was saying tightly, "Now, now, now," and Nora was racing into the light that came to meet her like the light through Gregory's telescope when he aimed it at the distant stars.

KERRY BECAME AWARE of her breathing and his own. He was floating, glowing.

"That game is going to be an instant bestseller," Nora predicted somewhat breathlessly.

"What game?" he asked, kissing her lightly.

"The one that says we don't have anything in common."

"We do too have something in common," he said, blowing lightly in her ear.

She shuddered, and thumped him between the shoulder blades. "Keep that up and this liaison's days are numbered."

"Is that what we have—a liaison?" He considered a while, frowning. "I think we could come up with a better description. Why don't we take the game into your bedroom and have an in-depth examination of the subject?"

She pushed him away and sat up, looking wonderfully disheveled and rosy. "No," she said firmly. "You and I have to talk. You've got to stop just turning up here when you feel like it. It's very... disturbing."

"I'm glad to hear that." He stroked his mustache in a way that suggested a silent-movie villain. His green eyes could look more wicked than any eyes Nora had ever seen. They apparently contained a lighting system that operated independently of any outside illumination. Coupled with that puckish face and droopy mustache, the effect was irresistibly comic when he wanted it to be.

Nora forced down the laughter that automatically bubbled up when she looked at him. "I'm serious, Kerry. I'm afraid Gregory's getting too fond of you."

He struck his forehead with an open palm. "How terrible. How did it happen? Was it something I did?"

Nora shook her head. "It may sound silly to you, Kerry, but he's had his heart broken more than once by some man who made a fuss of him and paid attention to him, then dropped him because things didn't work out with me."

Kerry nodded solemnly. "Your father told me you hadn't shown much sense in your choice of men both before and after your divorce."

"My father had no business telling you anything of the sort."

"Even though it's true?"

Nora sighed. "Even though it's true."

"That's why we should finish playing the Matchmaker game. If we find out we're all wrong for each other, we can simply go our separate ways and never bother each other again."

"You see, that's what I mean," Nora said hotly, covering up the fact that the bottom had dropped out of her stomach when he talked so casually of never seeing her again. "You could just walk out of here and leave Gregory wondering what he'd done to lose your friendship."

"Not at all," he said easily. "Gregory's my friend. I'd still come to visit him. Besides, I have to check up on Rusty at least once a week. I've never let a pup go out of the family before."

She eyed him rather cynically. "Are you telling me that if we get tired of, well, *seeing* each other . . . if we decide to call it quits, you'd keep up your friendship with Gregory?"

"And Lillian and Charles," he said. "And you. You have my word on it."

Somehow that thought was very comforting. "You're quite a guy, Kerry Ryan."

A mischievous, movie-villain light glowed once more in his eyes. He put one hand on her cheek and turned her head toward him, lining up her face for another kiss. "That, darling Nora . . ." he said softly, ". . . is what I've been trying to tell you."

7

IT WAS RAINING in Portland. It had rained throughout most of June. Sitting at the head of the conference table while his board of directors argued at the tops of their voices, Kerry cast a jaundiced eye at the dripping evergreens outside and the drizzle running down the floor-to-ceiling windows. He wished he was in California. In San Francisco, to be specific.

The thought worried him. He was getting far too wrapped up in thoughts of Nora Courtney. She didn't just pop up in his mind anymore, she *lived* in his mind. He'd even dreamed about her a couple of times lately. Not erotic dreams—he wouldn't have minded those— but domestic dreams that featured the two of them painting the lodge's window frames, which certainly needed paint . . . dreams of the two of them barbecuing chicken over the brick-and-metal grill he'd built on the lodge's patio . . . dreams of the three of them, Gregory leading the way, jogging along the beach under a cloudless sky, dogs running eagerly at their heels.

"A dollar for your thoughts," his mother said, leaning forward in the chair next to his around the corner of the table.

He lifted an eyebrow. "Inflation?"

"Nope. I just thought that as you were presently wearing your corporate-president hat, I should put a higher value on your thoughts than a penny."

He sighed. "I'm not sure what their value is, Ma." He cocked an eye at the rest of the people in the room. "Would you say they are winding down yet?"

His four sisters had strong opinions on everything and didn't believe in keeping their opinions to themselves. Their four husbands, although Kerry had characterized them to Nora as pussycats, were far from weaklings. Usually they disagreed with their wives and with each other. This volatile mixture made for interesting discussions, but little progress toward agreement.

Kate grinned as she surveyed her brood. She was beautifully dressed this morning, Kerry noted. Her creamy linen suit followed every curve of her sensational figure, and a green blouse made a glory of her eyes, aided by a slash of green eyeliner that Cleopatra would have admired. Kate Ryan might be fifty-five years old and her light brown hair might be "assisted" as she readily admitted, but she could definitely hold her own among her beautiful and no-less-statuesque daughters.

"At any other time I would enjoy the sight of my loved ones squabbling," she said. "Constructive squabbling is very healthy in a family. But I do have a hot lunch date with a warm-blooded doll designer," she added, dimpling, "so I'd just as soon we'd adjourn if it's all the same with you. Jump in, lovey, why don't you, and see what happens."

Kerry nodded. Tom Seaforth, Molly's husband, was speaking. "We've reached a stage where we have to grow. Look what happened to Mattel. Ruth and Elliott Handler founded it in the forties and by the early seventies the company was making a hundred and fifty million a year. Then Ray Wagner took over as president and boosted sales to the six-hundred-million-dollar level."

"I wouldn't mind us making six hundred million," Molly said dreamily.

"Would you buy another wig?" Brenda asked slyly, referring to a time in Molly's teens when she'd purchased a hairpiece, with disastrously embarrassing results.

Molly blew an inelegant raspberry at her twin.

"Maybe it's time for us to go public," Bridget suggested, as she always did.

"If we go public we'll be gobbled up by one of the big manufacturers in no time," Brenda's husband Roy said, as *he* always did. "If we need to increase profits we should consider a line of military models...tanks, ships. There's renewed interest this year in toy stores across the country."

"No war toys," Kate said before Kerry could, which earned her a grateful smile from her son.

"Military toys aren't the issue right now, anyway," Kerry said, jumping in as instructed. "The issue is the fact that our premises here have become woefully inadequate. The buildings are old and barely up to code anymore. We have to rebuild. Question is, do we build here or elsewhere? And do we expand at the same time?"

"It sure seems to me that we're making enough money," Colleen's husband Carter said. Kerry flashed him a surprised glance. It was the first opinion Carter had offered since joining the family. There might be hope for him, Kerry thought.

"There's no such thing as enough money," Jordan Lambert declaimed, stroking his piratical black beard as though he was the original wise philosopher.

Colleen smiled sweetly at him. "Bouncing on your head on Lombard Street did a whole lot for you, Jordan. You're in definite danger of becoming profound."

Lombard Street. San Francisco. Nora.

"Children, children," Kerry said with a sigh. "I don't know about you guys, but I'm getting hungry and—" He broke off as the conference room door opened and Lila Armitage's dark head appeared. "What is it, Lila?"

"Miss Greta Mallory is here to see you, Kerry," she said with a smirk.

Wolf whistles and catcalls greeted the announcement. "Great timing," Jordan commented. "Kerry just said he was hungry."

Kerry grinned and stroked his mustache suggestively for Jordan's benefit. Greta Mallory was the fabrics expert who was working with Toys Unlimited on the mass production of a synthetic fur that so far seemed destined for smashing success. As he had told the Courtneys, she was also a very sexy lady—a five-foot ten-inch brunette with violet eyes like Elizabeth Taylor's, and a figure like an old-fashioned egg timer with all of its sand in the right places.

When she had produced her first sample of mock seal fur she had suggested that Kerry come and examine it in her Seattle laboratory. Invited into the back room of an old warehouse, which she had converted into a studio apartment for nights when she worked late, Kerry had discovered that she'd spread the huge piece of white fake fur like a rug in front of a blazing log fire. When he turned to express his surprise, she was calmly removing her clothing. "I have an idea for a game that might interest you," she had murmured.

"As I was about to announce—" Kerry stood up as Lila retreated from the room, "—it's time for lunch." Ignoring the subsequent hoots of ribald laughter, he went on sternly. "I would suggest that you all present your recommendations in writing before July 4, and we'll discuss them immediately following the holiday." He hesitated, waiting for the groans to subside. They'd all rather argue than put together cogent and properly reasoned opinions, but they would do it anyway, and do it well. "By the way," he added, "I'll be entertaining visitors at the lodge for the Fourth of July weekend. I hope you'll understand."

"No way," Bridget objected.

"We always get together at the lodge for the Fourth," Colleen wailed. "This is Carter's first time. I promised him...."

Molly and Brenda spoke in chorus, as they often did. "Forget it, Kerry, it's our lodge too."

Kerry glowered at Brenda. "You weren't even going to be there until the Sunday," he pointed out. "You said you had to go to Roy's brother's place this year."

"What difference does that make?" she asked, with a lack of logic that was typical of all his sisters.

"You can't break with tradition," Kate said. "The girls would be terribly disappointed."

"The girls" were her granddaughters, Kerry's nieces.

Kerry looked at her pleadingly. "Ma . . ."

"What visitors are we talking about anyway?" she asked.

"My friend Nora and her son. From San Francisco. I told you about her."

"The John Simpson Bradford lady?"

Irritated, he said, "I wouldn't describe her that way. She doesn't belong to John Simpson Bradford."

Kate regarded him alertly. "I didn't realize you had a special interest in her. I thought this was just another casual . . ." She narrowed her eyes as he continued glowering at her. "My my, I'll be very interested to meet your Nora."

"She's not my Nora. She's just . . . a friend."

"Is that so? Well, I'll still be interested. All the same, I'm sorry, Son, but I'm afraid I agree with your sisters. The lodge is for all of us on the Fourth of July weekend, though your friend Nora is welcome, of course." She grinned at the others, who had been listening to this exchange in unaccustomed silence. "I can't wait to meet Kerry's friend myself," she said with a devilish wink. "How about the rest of you?"

There was an immediate chorus of agreement, interspersed with laughter.

"I thought I was supposed to be the head of this family," Kerry said, which brought a few more hoots his way. "Okay, we all go," he said with a sigh, wondering what Nora would think of his boisterous family. In town they were anything but subdued; at the beach they acted like kids let out of school, or frisky animals escaping from a zoo.

Why did what Nora think matter so much to him? He'd never worried about how his family would strike anyone. His attitude had always been: here we are, take us or leave us. He frowned, pondering all of this, then brightened as he remembered that Greta Mallory was waiting in his office. Greta Mallory was just the person to cure him of Nora Courtney. He pondered that thought, too. Why refer to Nora as though she were some kind of illness, maybe even a terminal illness? As he threw papers into his briefcase and headed for the door, he decided not to worry about it. Whatever the reason for his fears concerning Nora Courtney, the fact remained that Greta Mallory was guaranteed to take his mind off anybody and anything. He just might not be seen again for the rest of the day.

"YOU'D BETTER TOSS some more potatoes and onions into that chowder, ladies," Kate Ryan said as she looked out the lodge's kitchen window. "Brenda and Roy just drove in with their three girls." She chuckled. "They apparently made a successful getaway from Roy's brother's house."

Nora obediently dug out five more Idaho potatoes from the sack at her feet, and started peeling. On the other side of the butcher-block counter, Molly sliced a huge onion and suggested they'd better throw in another fish or two. This brought an argument from Kate, who said they were just supposed to be having Sunday lunch, for heaven's sake, and she'd already put enough fish in the huge pans of chowder to choke a whale.

Kate's comment provoked a joking response about Roy's appetite from Jordan, who was counting out wieners and ears of corn, which the nieces and Gregory were going to roast on the enormous bed of charcoal that Kerry and Bridget had arranged in the patio grill. There were still a few blueberry pies left from the staggering number Colleen and Carter had prepared, they being reputed to have the lightest touches with pastry. Kerry and Bridget—apparently they were very close to each other—had boned and filleted the fish. And Molly's husband, Tom, had made a trip into Seaside to buy more mayonnaise, more hot-dog buns, more relish, more mustard—all supplies having been used up on Friday and Saturday.

Every meal since Nora arrived had been as chaotic as this. The sheer logistics boggled her mind. Yet somehow everything always got cooked in time, everyone shared the work, nobody complained except in a joking way, which always led to more jokes and insults. In spite of their obvious love for one another, they were all great on insults.

Nora, though exhausted from laughing and working and jogging and Frisbee-chasing, wasn't sure if she'd ever had as much fun in her entire life, though the weekend certainly hadn't turned out the way she'd expected. Kerry had told her at the last minute that some of his family would be joining them at the lodge—all of them by the final day—but she hadn't really prepared herself for the reality of twelve exuberant people and five energetic dogs, six counting Rusty. That made seventeen people with the newcomers . . . no, *nineteen* with her and Gregory. She reached for two more potatoes.

"I couldn't talk them out of it, Nora," Kerry had told her on the telephone, sounding exasperated. "It's traditional that we go to the lodge for the Fourth and for Thanksgiving, and Ma insists that's the way it has to be."

"I don't mind at all, Kerry," she'd told him. "Why do you? Don't you get along with your family?"

He had sounded astonished. "I adore my family. It's just that, well, they're unpredictable."

"Pot calling the kettle black," Nora murmured.

"I've no idea how they'll treat you. They'll like you, how could they not? But they're all such jokers...." He'd sighed deeply. "I wish they weren't going to be there."

"Don't worry about it, Kerry," she'd told him, still not sure why he was so upset.

Now she thought she understood and wondered how she could have been so blind. Including a woman in a traditional family event could be seen as a fairly serious move. Kerry's family had certainly seen it that way. They had questioned her in subtle and not-so-subtle ways about her background, present circumstances and prospects ever since Kerry had flown her and Gregory up from San Francisco. They had attached great significance to the fact that Kerry had given Gregory one of his precious dogs, and they had exchanged meaningful glances whenever Kerry so much as handed her a dinner roll.

No wonder Kerry had felt nervous.

"So you're Nora."

She had been warned that Brenda was an exact duplicate of Molly, but even so she found herself looking unbelievingly across the counter at Molly to check that she really was still there and not here shaking her hand. She had been amazed to find that all the Ryan women and girls had eyes as blindingly green as Kerry's, and the same wickedly amused expressions. This resemblance was even more incredible. "Wow," she said.

"Molly and I are impressive, aren't we?" Brenda said with a laugh after she'd introduced Nora to Sandy, Missy and Joanne—who were all three as pretty and friendly and green-eyed as their cousins—and shooed them off to the beach to play with the other kids. "Once in a while one of us tries a new hairstyle or something to set us apart," she went on, "but we don't feel comfortable with the change and we go right back to looking like two peas in the genetic pod. As for clothes—" she gestured down at her khaki drill shorts and loosely knitted cotton top, which seemed to be a family uniform, "—we try to vary them in town, but usually it doesn't matter what I decide to wear, Molly always has the same thing on when I run into her."

ESP, Nora thought. She's heard it often existed between twins. Should she quote this instance to John the unbeliever? She pushed the thought of her boss away. She wasn't going to think of him. He was becoming too big a problem, and she had erased problems from her mind this weekend.

A deep male voice interrupted her musing. "Kerry Ryan's Nora, I presume?"

A former professional football player, Roy Delaney was even taller than Kerry and just as fair, though his features were heavier, his face ruddier and his body stockier than Kerry's. He also had a fair-sized paunch pushing against the belt of his chinos, which explained Jordan's crack about his appetite. "I salute Kerry's taste in women," Roy said with an openly admiring grin. "Then again, I always have."

"Roy!" his wife protested.

"Nora's not so naive as to think Kerry never had anything to do with another woman," Roy said, obviously uncowed.

"You could use a little tact," Kate said.

Roy grinned at his mother-in-law, swiped a piece of raw onion from Molly's pile, and popped it into his mouth. "Oh yeah? Who was it told that last girl, Sylvia was it?—the one who said she despised canned carrots—that she was as bad as Antoinette who asked if there was sugar in the gravy."

Kate looked sheepish. "Well, I believe in proper nutrition, but I can't stand health-food fanatics. Sylvia wanted me to serve alfalfa sprouts to this crowd," she informed Nora. "Can you imagine the reaction? Antoinette, who looked about as sturdy as a thistledown, ate mostly bee pollen." She shook her head. "Luckily they didn't either of them last long with Kerry," she said with satisfaction.

"They never do," Molly said cheerily.

Roy hooted. "Speaking of tact . . ." He swiped another piece of onion and headed for the living room.

"All of you Delaneys get to wash the dishes," Molly called after him, evidently trying to draw attention away from her own embarrassment. "That's what you get for arriving too late to help cook."

"Gotcha," he called over his shoulder.

"I'd wash a million dishes to get away from Roy's brother's house," Brenda said, following him out. "That sister-in-law of his and her immaculate housekeeping…aargh!" She stopped in the doorway, turned and squinted at Nora. "You don't wash doorknobs every day, do you?" she asked with sudden suspicion.

"I've never washed a doorknob in my life." Nora raised a hand as though she were in court.

"You'll do," Brenda said.

Turning to go through the dining room, she bumped into Kerry. "Who'll do what?" he asked, hugging her while keeping his charcoal-blackened hands away from her cotton sweater.

She hugged him back. "Nora will do," she explained. "I like her already."

"Good," he said, with a grin for Nora that set her nerve ends buzzing. But a moment later the hunted expression that was beginning to become familiar had reappeared on his face. Ever since they'd arrived here he'd kept glancing at her and chewing on his lower lip as though something were really vexing him.

Nora glanced at him from time to time as he washed his hands in the kitchen sink, trying not to be too obvious about it. What on earth was wrong? Was he wishing he hadn't invited her? "All the bathrooms are wall-to-wall nieces," he complained to his mother when she grumbled that he was getting in her way. He sounded cheerful enough, but his family's presence was definitely inhibiting him, Nora thought.

They hadn't spent any time alone together since he picked her and Gregory and Rusty up in San Francisco on the morning of the fourth. Bridget and Jordan and their two girls had flown up with them and they'd all arrived just in time to fix lunch. They'd all spent the afternoon on the beach, fixed an enormous dinner, watched the fireworks Tom and Carter had assembled, played a last game of Frisbee in the dark, then tumbled into their separate beds.

Nora had fully expected on Saturday that Kerry would try to inveigle her away from the others for a walk on the beach—perhaps a reprise of their burr-picking incident—especially when lowering clouds had set the stage for a spectacular sunset, followed by evening moonlight that bestowed a glamorous carpet of silver on the beach. But Kerry's sisters and brothers-in-law and even the nieces had watched them like hawks, and Kerry had evidently decided not to give them any excuse to jump to conclusions. Both nights Nora had slept in the women's dorm, Kerry in the men's, when he and Gregory finally tired of studying the night sky through Gregory's telescope. Kate, and Colleen and Carter—the newlyweds—had used the rooms Nora and Kerry had occupied before.

Of course, Kerry had been kept pretty busy. At one time or another, she had noticed, each of his sisters had turned up at Kerry's side, tugging on his arm, coaxing him into sitting with her in a corner or on the patio or the beach so she could talk to him in private, her head close to his, her gaze fixed on his face while he responded. Their husbands were just as likely to turn to him for advice on anything from a tangled fishing reel to a splinter lodged under a fingernail to a car whose battery had died.

The nieces also hung around their uncle. Last night he'd gathered them all in front of the fire and told them tall tales about America's frontier. They had all, with Gregory in their midst, listened without interrupting once. This morning little Maggie, Molly's youngest, had brought him a toy truck to repair; Bridget's Debbie, the eldest niece, had asked him to fix the lock on her diary. "You're the only one I can trust not to read it," she'd told him solemnly.

Yet even though they all obviously adored him, none of the nieces had minded when Kerry included Gregory in their games. And they had gone along with Kerry's suggestion that Gregory be inducted into the family as an honorary member. "He's even got green eyes," he'd pointed out, with a grin for Nora. There had been a small ceremony, over which Kerry had presided solemnly. Gregory had been presented with a green and white Toys Unlimited T-shirt which hadn't left his body since.

No doubt about it, she thought as she wiped down her section of cutting board, Kerry Ryan was a family man. Which meant that even if he didn't know it, or wouldn't admit it, he was probably also the marrying kind. In theory, all she had to do was point that out to him. She sighed. In practice, nothing was ever that simple.

Kerry glanced worriedly at her as he dried his hands. His tan had darkened since they'd arrived here. His mustache was almost the same color as his skin. There were lines in his forehead she hadn't noticed before. She wanted to take his hand and lead him to the nearest bedroom, wrap her arms around him, kiss him until they were both breathless, then ask him if she'd offended him in some way. "Have you noticed that Gregory's in love?" he asked.

Nora smiled ruefully. "With Molly and Tom's daughter Pat. Yes, I've noticed. How old is she? Twelve?"

"Thirteen." His face had cleared. "You don't mind then? I thought you might worry that he was acting beyond his years again. Not that you need to. Pat's a terrific kid. She's a good friend for him. She knows a lot about tidal pools."

Nora nodded. "Gregory adores anyone who can teach him things. And I'm certainly not worried about him. He's having a good time." An understatement. She had never seen Gregory look so happy. "I love it here, Mom," he'd told her not an hour ago. It wasn't the place he was referring to, Nora knew, though the place was certainly spectacularly beautiful . . . it was the family he meant.

Kerry studied her face as he carefully hung the towel on a nearby rack. "How about you?" he asked. "Are you having a good time too?"

She felt rather than saw that everyone else in the room was anxiously awaiting her answer. What thoroughly nice people they were under all the badinage. "I'm a little weak from laughing and too much jogging on the sand, but otherwise things couldn't be better," she said. But that wasn't quite true. Things could be a lot better. She could be wrapped warmly, securely, in Kerry's arms.

He grinned wickedly, becoming for a moment the familiar Kerry who hadn't been around the last couple of days, the Kerry who had stolen her heart. "You think you're weak now, wait until we play volleyball after lunch."

"We're all champion volleyball players," Kate crowed.

Nora groaned, and they all laughed. She felt warm all the way through, she realized, and not just because the chowder pots were steaming or because the sun was shining on the beach outside. This was the kind of warmth that was associated with home and hearth and family. She felt accepted.

She wanted this, she decided as she was leaping and lunging with the best of them on Kerry's side of the volleyball net. She wanted all of it—the jokes, the insults, the laughter, the energy. She wanted this rowdy, vital, wonderful family for herself and for Gregory. Above all else, she wanted Kerry Ryan—wit, raconteur, doctor, friend, brother, head of the family... lover...wanted him for keeps, wanted him so badly she ached.

LESS THAN AN HOUR after she'd allowed this decision to form in her mind, the sky fell in on her. Feeling sweaty but happy, she had gone up to the women's bathroom to wash some of the sand off herself. Kerry was going to fly her and Gregory home in an hour or so. He would be returning to Oregon immediately, as he had an important board meeting the next day. "Lots of meetings ahead, too," he'd told her. "We have some important decisions to make. I may not be too available for a while."

That was really rather an ominous statement, she thought briefly, but she felt too relaxed and pleasantly weary to worry about it.

Brushing her hair, she became aware that Molly and Brenda were in the dormitory on the other side of the bathroom wall, evidently sitting on their beds which were at this end of the long room. A few seconds later she realized that they didn't know she was anywhere nearby.

"I like her," Molly was saying. "She fits right in. No airs and graces about her. She didn't mind a bit sleeping in the dorm and nobody had to ask her to help with anything, she just dug right in. She's smart too. Of course, Kerry wouldn't ever be interested in a dumb woman, but she's even brighter than average, and that boy of hers is a wonder. In ten years we'll be bragging that we knew him when."

According to the old maxim, eavesdroppers weren't supposed to hear good things about themselves, Nora thought even as she moved closer to the wall. It would be embarrassing all around if she revealed herself now, she rationalized. In truth, nothing could have torn her away.

"She's in love with Kerry," Brenda said. "It shows on her face every time she looks at him. Poor kid. You think there's any chance Kerry could be serious about her?" Now that she couldn't see the twins, Nora found she could easily distinguish between them. Brenda's voice was just a little lower than Molly's, and perhaps a little more musical.

Molly laughed. "Kerry? You talking about our brother Kerry?"

"He seems nervous, and not as zany as usual. Listen, he actually kept an honest score in the volleyball match . . . he didn't cheat once."

"You're right. Something's terribly wrong."

"I'm serious, Moll. It would be so great if Kerry would fall for someone like Nora. I sometimes think he's lonely."

Molly hooted with laughter. "He wasn't lonely on Wednesday."

There was a moment's silence during which something cold clutched at Nora's stomach. She suddenly wished fervently that she had made her presence known the moment she heard Brenda's voice. But she certainly couldn't escape now; the only way out was through the dorm.

Brenda giggled. "You mean Greta Mallory? The rug lady?"

Kerry's fabrics expert, Nora remembered. The sexy lady who had brought a smile of reminiscence to his face when he told Lillian about her fake seal fur.

"You heard that story, too?" Molly asked. "It was supposed to be a secret. Kerry only told it to Jordan. Jordan told Bridget of course, and she told me in strictest confidence. Gosh, I've been so virtuous keeping my mouth shut, and you knew it all the time."

"Did Bridget tell you that the first time Kerry went to see Greta's fake fur rug, she took all her clothes off and offered herself up like a human sacrifice? Kerry was never in his life so taken aback. Not enough to turn her down, of course."

"Do you suppose she did it again on Wednesday?"

"It's possible. Kerry was gone all afternoon." Brenda giggled again. "Would she bring her rug with her, do you suppose?"

"Have rug will travel," Molly quipped, and they both dissolved into laughter.

A moment later Nora heard bedsprings creak and she tensed, afraid one of them might want to use the bathroom. But the two sets of footsteps went in the opposite direction.

As soon as the sound faded away, Nora hurried out of the bathroom and up the stairs to the next floor. She went out onto the balcony where Kerry and Gregory had studied the moon and stars the previous night. She leaned on the railing and took a much needed breath of salt-scrubbed air, feeling vaguely sick. Old maxims were usually right, she conceded. She would feel much better if she hadn't heard any of that sisterly conversation.

Greta Mallory didn't sound like the type any man would take seriously, of course. The problem was that the twins had been referring to some incident that had taken place just last Wednesday. Kerry's relationship with Greta, whatever it was, was not ancient history.

A burst of laughter down below drew her gaze to the group still playing volleyball on the grass beyond the patio. Kerry had lifted Gregory to his shoulders so that he could return some of the higher balls. Her son was clutching Kerry's forehead with one arm, attempting to punch the ball with the other amid cries of foul. The sun was shining on both of them, making aureoles around their heads . . . one fair, one dark. Gregory was laughing uproariously.

Watching the two of them, she felt as though her heart was going to break. She should have known that Kerry Ryan was too good to be true.

No. She was not going to pass judgment on Kerry on hearsay. When the opportunity arose she would ask him about Greta Mallory, find out what he had to say. After a while, when the feeling of betrayal wasn't so strong in her. After a while, when she could be casual about the whole thing. After a while, when the pain was no longer so sharp.

8

DURING THE SUMMER MONTHS in San Francisco, fog frequently creeps in from the Pacific, drawn from the ocean by hot air rising inland from the Nevada Desert and the valleys of the Sierra Nevada mountains. Fog-horns cry out in a lonely chorus. Swirling at first, then rolling, the fog advances steadily, bleaching the color from the houses and the flowers in the carts on Union Square, veiling the tall buildings in mystery, turning the city gray. In the days that followed the July 4th week-end, as Nora racketed up and downhill on her beloved cable cars, jogged in Golden Gate Park with Gregory and Rusty, watched a sidewalk entertainer while eating her lunch in a streetside plaza, drove up the hill to her parents' house, or rode the Airporter back and forth to the occasionally socked-in airport, her mood matched the foggy weather.

She spent the night hours sorting through her emotions as though they were dirty laundry. This wounded feeling wasn't jealousy, she decided. It was more like disappointment, heavily lined with injured pride. How could Kerry get involved, even momentarily, with someone like Greta Mallory while he was supposedly, even if loosely, involved with her?

She still intended to ask him about Greta next time she was alone with him. She wasn't quite sure how she would go about it. She could hardly come right out and accuse him melodramatically of cheating on her. After all, he was a free agent. He hadn't promised her anything. He had told her right at the start that he was a determined bachelor, a man who avoided concepts like "happily ever after" and "playing for keeps."

Kerry, of course, had no idea that she knew about Greta, and he continued sending her comic cards that played on words and made fun of the relationship between men and women. He was busy and so was she, but as soon as they had some free time he would come to town again and take her out, he told her cheerfully on the telephone, apparently not noticing that she was practically monosyllabic. He was thinking about her problem with John Simpson Bradford...he was sure he'd come up with a solution eventually.

Nora managed somehow to function with her usual efficiency. But whenever she reached the point in one of her seminars where she said, "and in conclusion," another phrase echoed sonorously in her brain, like the title of a scary movie...the beginning of the end.

When John reminded her from time to time that he was still waiting patiently for her answer, she found herself seriously considering the merits of his proposal. Obviously her judgment of men was impaired...her own deeper feelings couldn't be trusted to choose a new father for Gregory. Theoretically, she could certainly do a lot worse than marry John Simpson Bradford.

Kerry came to town on the third Sunday in July. There was no fog that day. For once he called first, suggesting dinner out. But being Kerry, he had to do *something* unpredictable. This time he brought his mother with him. Nora heard the two of them greeting her parents in the downstairs foyer and wondered why he'd brought Kate along. Maybe he still didn't want to be alone with her.

Kate looked wonderful in a kelly green velvet suit that fitted her like a second skin. Kerry looked magnificent and unusually elegant in a navy blazer, gray slacks, white shirt and dark tie. His hair and mustache were newly trimmed. Nora's heart seemed to swell out toward him when she came down the stairs to welcome them, but then as she remembered Greta Mallory and her fake fur rug it contracted inside her chest like a balloon whose air had leaked out through a pinhole.

"You look lovely, Nora," Kerry said as she came toward him. "That dress is the exact color of your eyes. Grand Marnier. Is there such a color?"

"I don't think so, but it's a nice compliment. Thank you."

He seemed surprised at the stiffness in her voice. For a moment she was tempted to wipe the surprise off his face by saying flat out, "I hear you had a visit from Greta Mallory," but she managed to restrain herself. She wasn't quite ready to force any kind of confrontation. She was so afraid that the hearsay would turn out to be true. As long as she didn't know for sure, she could pretend, she could hope . . .

Turning to Kate as Kerry frowned, she said brightly, "Kate, it's wonderful to see you. I'm so glad you came. I've wanted my folks to meet you."

She was not surprised by the fact that Lillian and Charlie were immediately captivated by Kate Ryan. Nor was it surprising that Gregory was thrilled to see her when Nora brought them both upstairs. Kate had a way with children that was not grandmotherly but conspiratorial, as though she and they were in league against the boring rules and regulations of the world. "My kids always try to get rid of me, too, whenever anything interesting's going on," she sympathized when Nora suggested Gregory should go tackle his homework. "Why don't I come with you and take a look through this telescope Kerry's been telling me about."

"You can visit with Rusty, too," Gregory said excitedly, leading the way. Rusty had been barking right along, probably because he'd recognized the voices of his former owners.

"Is this a business trip?" Nora asked when Kate returned a few minutes later with a squirming Rusty in her arms.

"No," Kate said. Tucking Rusty under one arm, she accepted a cocktail from Nora and settled herself comfortably on the sofa.

"In a way," Kerry said, standing with his back to the empty fireplace.

Nora looked from one to the other. "Which?" she asked.

Kate laughed and took a sip of her Tanqueray-and-tonic. Rusty had draped himself across her lap and closed both eyes in blissful contentment. "As far as I'm concerned, my son invited me to dinner in San Francisco," Kate said. "It's not my birthday for another couple of months, but I never refuse a free meal. There were times in my childhood when I could have used one. I didn't even know I was coming here, to your house, Nora. I'm happy to be here, you understand, but if Kerry's brought me here under false pretenses and there's no food in the offing, I may have to put him over my knee and spank him soundly."

She and Nora exchanged grins at the prospect. Then they both looked inquiringly at Kerry. "I'm definitely taking you to dinner, Ma," he said, laughing. "I'm also taking Nora if she's still of a mind to come. And John Simpson Bradford also," he added after Nora nodded hesitantly.

Nora looked at him, narrow-eyed. "Why John?" she asked, seating herself beside Kate and ruffling one of Rusty's long copper-colored ears.

"Why me?" Kate asked with a groan.

"I told John you were in charge of the doll-making department at Toys Unlimited," Kerry said to his mother. He turned to Nora. "I called him at the office. He was delighted to hear from me, especially when I told him Ma was interested in hosting a seminar—like the one you gave our management people—for her employees. We're going to discuss the possibilities over dinner in the Garden Court of the Sheraton Palace Hotel. John's idea. He says he loves their Sunday buffet. One of the finest traditions in San Francisco, he says."

"That's funny," Kate murmured. "I don't remember requesting a seminar. Do you suppose I'm getting senile?"

"Not a chance," Nora said. She had an idea what Kerry might be up to, but whatever it was she didn't think she was going to like it. He was looking altogether too innocent, gazing now into the depths of his bourbon-and-water as though something wondrous was happening there.

"You could have arranged the seminar just as easily over the telephone," she pointed out. "Why come all this way for dinner with John?"

"It was his idea, Nora," he said defensively. "As I told him, this might lead to several more seminars. I might even mention how great they are at the next International Toy Fair."

"That would be very nice of you," Nora said suspiciously. "And I'm sure the manufacturers and their employees would benefit. But I'm not sure I believe all this is the reason for tonight's dinner. I have a definite feeling that you have mischief in mind. Does this dinner date have anything to do with my problem, by any chance?"

"What problem?" Kate asked.

"Mischief? Me?" Kerry looked at Nora over the rim of his glass, then took a sip, still managing to look virtuous. "I do want to help you with your problem, of course," he said blandly.

"What problem?" Kate asked again.

"You didn't have some crazy idea about matchmaking, did you?" Nora asked.

He had wandered over to the front window and was looking out. He didn't answer her. "Am I warm?" she prodded.

"Moderately so," he said. His voice sounded muffled, as though he might be laughing to himself.

"If someone doesn't tell me what problem we are talking about I'm going to scream," Kate said fiercely.

Nora inclined her head toward her, but kept her gaze fixed on Kerry over by the window. "John asked me to marry him about a month ago," she explained. "I told Kerry I was worried he might fire me if I turned him down. Kerry promised to come up with a solution to the problem."

"I'm confused," Kate said. "How will seeing you with Kerry and me persuade John to let you off the hook?" Her face cleared. "Oh, you said matchmaking. Are we supposed to pretend that you and Kerry are in love?" She shook her head. "If that's the way of it, why am I here? The two of you could be more convincing without me, I'm—" She looked at Nora with both eyebrows raised, then at Kerry who had turned around from the window and was watching her with a wide grin on his expressive face.

"You wouldn't," she said to her son. "You've not got some crazy idea of matching me up with John Simpson Bradford? It's Colleen who thinks he's God's gift to women, remember? And even she wouldn't look at him twice now that she's got Carter. You're out of your mind, Kerry Ryan. I've said all along that the man seems a bit pompous." She turned apologetically to

Nora. "I'm sorry, Nora dear, I know he's your employer, and maybe your friend, but all the same...."

"He is rather stuffy," Nora agreed. "I don't think he means to be, and he's undoubtedly a brilliant man. But as Gregory says, he's inclined to take himself too seriously. And unfortunately, he doesn't have a sense of humor."

"I'm not asking you to marry the man, Ma," Kerry said in a reasonable-sounding voice. "All you have to do is be nice to him for a couple of hours. Be yourself. Let him see there are other attractive women in the world besides Nora."

"It's a terrible idea," Nora said furiously before Kate could speak. "Talk about using people..."

The tone of her voice evidently disturbed Rusty, who lifted his head and looked at her, then jumped down to the floor and scooted over to Kerry, showing clearly whose side he was on.

Kerry bent down to pat the dog, and Rusty wriggled with pleasure. "I'm just trying to help," he said again.

Nora glared at him. "You can quit right now. Of all the nerve, to think that your own mother would..."

Again Rusty sat upright and looked at her, his ears drooping, then he barked once and scuttled out of the room and up the stairs to Gregory's attic, obviously in search of a more peaceful atmosphere. They all laughed, and some of the tension between them dissipated.

"You know, Nora," Kate said, touching her arm, "now that I understand what Kerry has in mind, I'm not that opposed." Her hand squeezed Nora's forearm gently and she winked broadly. Her back was turned to Kerry so he couldn't possibly see what was going on. She had some secret plan up her sleeve, obviously, and whatever it was, she wanted Nora to go along with her.

Cooperating, Nora subsided as Kate turned to Kerry and asked in a soft-as-velvet voice. "What exactly do you want me to do, lovey?"

He grinned, evidently scenting victory. "Nothing elaborate. What I thought would probably happen is this." He turned to Nora. "While we are talking about seminars Ma will flirt discreetly with John." He glanced sideways at Kate, then back to Nora. "She flirts with every male between nine and ninety, anyway. She can't help herself. If John Simpson Bradford has any red blood in his veins at all he'll flirt right back with her, and then you can tell him you can't marry a man who isn't single-minded about you. He'll be in the wrong, so he can hardly feel rejected."

"That's entrapment," Nora exclaimed. "It's an awful—" Kate once more exerted pressure on her arm.

"Awful smart idea," Kate said admiringly. "Kerry's quite right, Nora dear. I'm a terrible flirt. It will be good practice for me."

Once more, she winked broadly, then looked innocent when Kerry approached. Kerry gathered up their cocktail glasses. "Let's get this show on the road," he suggested happily over his shoulder as he took the glasses out to the kitchen.

Nora looked inquiringly at Kate. "You've got some mischief in mind yourself, haven't you?" she whispered.

"But of course, my dear," Kate Ryan said with a smile that was as devilishly wicked as her son's.

THOUGH IT WAS BILLED as the most beautiful dining room in the world, though it had hosted presidents and princes, the Garden Court at the Sheraton Palace Hotel was not one of Nora's favorite places to eat. The food was undoubtedly excellent, and she admired the elegance of the marble columns, the magnificently arching leaded-glass dome and the gigantic crystal chandeliers. But the vast echoing dining room reminded her of a nineteenth-century railway terminal, and she was always subconsciously expecting to hear someone announce stridently, over the mellow sounds of the string quartet, "All aboard." Given a choice, she would have preferred the cozier atmosphere of the Pied Piper room with its rich wood paneling and its Maxfield Parrish mural.

However, the Pied Piper was closed on weekends, and in any case she had not been given a choice of restaurant any more than she had been given a choice of table companions. If it hadn't been for Kate Ryan's magnificently outrageous behavior, she would have remained furious with Kerry Ryan the entire evening.

From the minute Kerry had introduced a demurely smiling Kate to John, it was obvious that Kate had made up her mind to teach her son a lesson by romancing John Simpson Bradford's socks off. Obvious to Nora and Kerry anyway, if not to John.

Within half an hour Kerry was embarrassed to death and was muttering to Nora, "Tell her to knock it off, I've got the picture. It was a lousy idea."

Nora couldn't even respond for fear of laughing out loud. Kate Ryan in action was awesome.

"And haven't I admired you from afar these many months," she had told John when he met them in the Sheraton Palace lobby. He was beautifully groomed as always, his dress-for-success clothing immaculate, his hair newly blow-dried, his gold-rimmed glasses shining.

Kate was too tall to look up at him, so instead she had looked directly into his dazzled eyes, batting her long lashes at him. "Oh, how very nice this is," she'd sighed, slipping her hand daintily under John's arm when he offered to escort her into the dining room. "There's a whole difference in the way a mature man such as yourself takes care of a lady. Those of us who are also mature appreciate such courtesies." She patted his arm with her free hand. "Such a strong man," she'd murmured. John had actually clenched his fist so that his bicep would stand out a little more. Nora had been afraid to meet Kerry's eyes.

Once they had all served themselves from the sumptuous buffet, Kate had drawn John out to talk about his entire life and the origins of the John Simpson Bradford Seminars. She hung on his every word, when she wasn't exclaiming and admiring in the thick brogue she'd dug up from somewhere.

"Can you believe the intellect of him, then?" she demanded of Nora and Kerry, palms spread, green eyes dramatically wide with amazement. "'Tis men like John who inspire multitudes to climb the Himalayas in search of enlightenment. Oh, 'tis a wonder indeed," she added to John, leaning in to him so close that her magnificent breasts almost brushed the lapels of his pinstripe suit. "To think that you invented this entire concept your own self and molded it into an American success story. Oh, I can't wait to try out your methods. I've always admired those women who have everyone's attention the moment they walk into a room. I just know you'll be teaching me how to project a stronger image, and how to make people hear my voice on the job."

"Heaven help us all," Kerry muttered.

John's eyes looked glazed. He was lapping up the praise. Nora didn't really blame him. What human being could withstand such flattery? He did once mutter something about Dale Carnegie and Norman Vincent Peale, so he wasn't too far gone to give a little credit where it was due; still, he was obviously enjoying his new role as the Guru of the Western World.

"Ma," Kerry whispered when John's attention was temporarily diverted by a wine steward. "I didn't tell you to lay it on with a trowel."

Kate's green eyes flashed merrily and unrepentantly in his direction for the space of a second. "I can't help myself," she said, reminding him of what he'd said to Nora. Then she fixed her gaze again on John's bemused face and placed one hand delicately over his where it lay on the table. "Tell me some more about women's opportunites for human growth and potential in the business world today," she begged. "I love the way those wonderful phrases roll off your inspired tongue."

By the time dinner was over, John had obviously forgotten Nora and Kerry were even present. His face was flushed, his eyes mesmerized by Kate's adoring green gaze. He was obviously enchanted by her. He would conduct the seminar for her employees himself, he assured her as they waited for the valet service to bring his Mercedes around. Just as soon as he checked his calendar he would call her and arrange a time.

Nora had to admire the skillful way Kate avoided John's offer to drive her and Kerry to Russian Hill where they were staying with Bridget and Jordan. With one last lingering flutter of her impossibly long eyelashes, she assured him she would prefer to carry in her memory the thought of him driving away in his powerful automobile while she waved from the sidewalk. He actually looked flattered by this suggestion as he gallantly kissed her hand, seemingly unaware that he had been dismissed in masterful fashion.

"Until we meet again," Kate murmured, as he settled himself reluctantly behind the steering wheel.

"I don't believe this farewell scene," Nora said in tones of awe as the Mercedes drew majestically away and Kate fluttered a handkerchief where John could see it in the rearview mirror. "I kept expecting John to say, 'Here's looking at you, kid.'"

"It did have overtones of Ingrid Bergman and Humphrey Bogart, didn't it?" Kate said demurely.

"You made an absolute exhibition of yourself all evening," Kerry charged indignantly.

"I did, didn't I?" Kate said with satisfaction and a glint in her eye that had appeared the moment John's car was out of sight. "Perhaps you'll think twice before offering your poor old mother up as a sacrifice in future."

"One," Kerry said heatedly. "No one with an ounce of imagination could describe you as my poor old mother. And two, I didn't tell you to come on to the man like some vamp out of a silent movie."

"You had no business dreaming up the whole idea in the first place," Nora said flatly. "Now your mother is stuck with a seminar she probably doesn't want, and a man who thinks she's the . . ."

"Bee's knees?" Kate supplied mischievously as Nora paused to think up a suitable description. "Cat's pajamas?" She chuckled. "Don't worry about the seminar, Nora," she said. "It won't hurt my bunch a bit to get some education. I wouldn't have gone so far if I hadn't thought the seminar was a good idea, believe me. I've heard enough about your marvelous seminar from Marnie and Lila and Ted Hutchins to know that John's concepts are sound." She hesitated, looking very thoughtful. "And actually," she added slowly, "I'm not so mad at Kerry as I was. I think John Simpson Bradford's rather a pet."

Nora stared at her speechlessly for a moment, all the wind taken out of her sails. "You do?"

"You must admit that not many men kiss your hand nowadays," Kate pointed out. "There's a certain old-fashioned charm in that."

"Ma," Kerry said tersely. "You surely aren't getting serious ideas about John Simpson Bradford?" He was still looking very stern, though the wind was playfully tousling his hair and lifting the ends of his tie.

Kate smirked at him. "It would serve you right if I was," she said. "But as it happens, I merely meant I wouldn't mind dating him. A single mature lady such as myself is forever in need of a presentable escort. However," she added, shaking her head at him, "as you of all people should surely know, I don't get serious ideas about any man. There was only ever one man for me in that way, and we all know who he was."

A sudden glory blazed in her face, and Kerry and Nora both stared at her in silence and perhaps homage for a moment. Her husband had died when Kerry was seventeen, Nora remembered. That was eighteen years ago. What a wonderful love it must have been to survive eighteen years of separation.

"Ma," Kerry said softly. His eyes were moist, and there was the most curious yearning expression on his face.

"Well," Nora said lamely, feeling rather at a loss. Then she turned on Kerry again in a deliberate attempt to lighten the atmosphere. "Your mother may have forgiven you," she said, "but I haven't. You had no business interfering. I'm perfectly capable of handling my own affairs."

Kerry frowned at her, looking so irresistibly, wonderfully little-boy macho that her heart turned a double somersault. "*I* wouldn't call you capable," he said irritably. "Did you tell John right away that it was out of the question for you to marry him? Did you remind him he's thirty years older than you?" He hesitated. "Anyway, I don't see why you're so mad at me. Didn't you ask me to come up with a solution to your problem?"

"I said let me know if you had any ideas. I didn't give you license to act on my behalf. If you'd brought up this idea sooner, before you fixed the date with John, I'd have vetoed it immediately."

"Would you now? And you'd still be waffling around in another month, I suppose, afraid to tell him no, keeping him in suspense waiting for your answer because you don't want to jeopardize your security. I suppose you think that's kind?"

"No, I don't think it's kind," Nora said. "I just want to find a way to tell him that won't hurt his feelings." She slanted a glance at Kate. "Anyway, this whole argument is academic now. I don't think John even noticed I was here this evening."

"He was rather taken with me, wasn't he?" Kate said serenely.

Kerry looked questioningly at Nora. "Don't tell me you were miffed because he ignored you?"

"Of course not," Nora said, but her voice lacked conviction.

Kerry let out an explosive breath. "I swear, with all the women around me, you'd think I'd have learned to understand them, but I never will. You wanted out the minute he proposed to you. You know you did."

"I still do," she said firmly.

"But you want to be the one to turn him down, right?" Kate said. "It's simple enough, Kerry. Women don't like rejection. If a relationship is to come to an end, they want to be the ones to end it." She patted Nora's arm. "I'm sorry, dear. I got carried away, I'm afraid."

"Carried away," Kerry echoed, suddenly remembering his own anger. "You can say that again. You had no business—"

Kate touched his arm and shook her head at him. "Enough, lovey. I'm getting chilly standing here. That wind must be coming straight off the ocean." She shivered charmingly and looked around. "Why don't I get that lovely young man over there to whistle us up a taxi so I can go put my poor old feet up and drink a cup of hot chocolate."

"I'll get us a taxi," Kerry said sternly. "I wouldn't trust you around any so-called lovely man for a minute."

Nora and Kate both giggled. "He's mad at both of us, wouldn't you say?" Kate whispered, as he headed for the corner to look for a cab.

"He's giving a fair imitation of it," Nora whispered back.

"Serves him right," Kate said.

In the cab, Kerry thought for a minute when the driver asked him "Where to?" He turned to look over his shoulder at the two women and suggested that he drop Kate off at the Lamberts and then take Nora home. "That's fine with me," Kate said cheerfully.

Nora's stomach contracted. It was one thing to decide she was going to bring up Greta Mallory casually the next time she was alone with Kerry, another actually to contemplate doing it. The moment they were alone, he would probably take her in his arms and she would forget completely that he'd had anything to do with another woman. And then she'd hate herself. She was not going to let him come to her from another woman's arms. Her pride would not allow that. "I have to go to work early tomorrow," she said hastily. "It would probably be better to drop me off first."

"You're still annoyed with me, aren't you?" Kerry said softly. "I'm sorry, Nora. If I offer my abject apologies to you and Ma...if I concede that tonight's get-together was a stupid idea, is there any chance you'll forgive me? I learned my lesson, believe me. Ma's antics taught me to keep my brighter ideas to myself. I promise never again to interfere in your life."

But I might want you to interfere in my life, Nora thought contrarily.

"Antics indeed!" Kate exclaimed with a sniff. Then she smiled. "Ah now, that's a fairly gracious apology, lovey, and all's well that ends well." She turned to Nora. "What do you say we forgive him? I think he's suffered enough."

"Okay," Nora said, managing a smile in Kerry's direction. "You're forgiven. For tonight's mischief, at least."

"There was more?" Kate asked, looking from Nora to Kerry. She shook her head. "Sorry. None of my business."

Nora looked directly at Kerry. That was a mistake. His green eyes were almost luminous in the dim interior of the taxi. He was such a beautiful, beautiful man. He was looking very perplexed. "What else is there, Nora? Surely we can straighten out whatever it is. *May* I take you home? I won't stay long." He hesitated, suddenly looking unusually solemn. "There's something I'd really like to talk to you about."

Her heart thumped against her ribs. What did he want to say to her? That it would be better if they never saw each other again? *Greta Mallory*, she reminded herself. *Have rug, will travel*. Had Nora Courtney been replaced . . . outclassed? "Maybe next time you're in town," she said lamely, delaying the inevitable.

After a moment in which he looked at her in silence, he nodded, then turned away and gave instructions to the cab driver.

Nora wondered if she would ever see him again.

9

JOHN WAS ILL AT EASE all morning. He kept coming into the front office where Nora was dictating notes on her most recent seminar to one of the secretaries, hovering for a couple of minutes, then smiling weakly when both women looked up at him. "Everything okay?" he asked each time, then left when they agreed there were no problems. A few minutes later he would repeat the whole sequence.

"Is everything okay with you?" Nora finally asked after the secretary left for lunch.

"Well, no, to tell you the truth, I'm not okay." He walked over to the window and peered through the pleated Verosol blind at a cable car struggling gamely and noisily up California Street. Nora could imagine the conductor jokingly telling the passengers to lean forward.

"I'm a little ashamed of the way I behaved last night," John continued.

Nora let a couple of minutes pass in silence. He really didn't deserve to be let off the hook right away.

At length, he turned from the window, looking like a small boy who knew he had to face the music but was reluctant to do so. "You must be very, very angry with me."

"I wouldn't say angry," she said, then added mischievously, "slighted, maybe. Verging on insulted. You did just ask me to marry you. I hadn't even told you—"

"Before you say anything more," he said hastily, "perhaps I ought to admit that I've had second, well, I've thought a little more deeply and it seems to me . . ." His voice trailed away, and he went back to peering through the blind again, leaning on the sill as though there were something terribly fascinating happening out there. As far as Nora could tell the busy street scene, though always interesting, was no more dramatic than usual.

"What exactly are you trying to say?" Nora asked, though of course she knew. Kerry's plan had worked, in a backhanded sort of way. And she was relieved— she hadn't relished hurting John's feelings. But damn it, what about *her* feelings? John hadn't considered them at all. No, she wasn't going to let him off easily.

Looking so sheepish that it was difficult for Nora to keep a straight face, John approached her and took both her hands between his. She was afraid he was going to fall to his knees and beg forgiveness. "I'm sorry, Nora," he said. "I realize I've behaved very badly all around. I neglected you totally last evening."

He took a deep breath, evidently gathering his courage. "I'm going to have to hurt you even more, Nora," he added gently. "I'm going to have to withdraw my proposal, and I'm not really sure I can explain why. I don't quite know what happened to me."

Nora knew what had happened to him. He had discovered that he was capable of passion after all. And he had liked it.

"I've never met anyone quite like Kate Ryan before," he muttered, looking altogether bewildered and arousing all Nora's sympathy.

"She's a wonder, isn't she?" Nora slipped her hands free and took hold of John's, patting them sympathetically. "There's something *you* should know, John. Kate was very happily married for quite a few years. Even though she's been widowed for a long time, I don't think she'd ever consider marrying again."

"So she told me."

Startled, Nora let go of his hands and stared at him. "You've talked to her since last night?"

"This morning. I called to invite her to breakfast. She asked for a rain check. She's going to call me next time she's in town, but she said, well, she made it fairly clear, in a casual sort of way, that she wasn't interested in anything serious."

He looked so glum that Nora's heart went out to him. "I'm sorry, John," she murmured.

His mournful eyes reminded her of Rusty's. "I must say you are taking this very well, Nora," he said gratefully. "I do want you to understand that I'm not as flighty as I may seem."

"I would never think of you as flighty, John," Nora said with complete sincerity.

"Thank you, Nora." Regret appeared in his eyes. "I really did think for a time that you and I . . ." He hesitated. "It was just that Kate, well, meeting Kate, made me realize that I need to loosen up a little in my lifestyle. That I should perhaps look around at women closer to my own age before I make any rash decisions."

Rash decisions, indeed. About to protest, Nora sighed instead. There wasn't much point in taking umbrage. Persuading John that marriage between them was out of the question had been the whole idea, hadn't it? She groaned as a thought occurred to her. "I suppose this means I'm not getting the transfer to head office either," she said mournfully.

John frowned down at her. "I didn't think it was all that important to you," he said. "I thought you liked traveling."

She had to be careful here or she could talk herself right out of a job. "I do like to get around," she said slowly. "It's just that Gregory needs me, you know." A devil entered her, making her voice sound just a little on the whining side. "When you, well, proposed to me, and said I could make my own hours and have my own office here, I naturally began to think of the benefits to Gregory...." She let her voice trail away as she looked sadly up into his eyes.

The twitch under his right eye had returned, fueled by guilt this time rather than nervousness. He had gripped her shoulder as though to encourage her to hang in there, not to break down. "I do feel badly about Gregory," he said.

Thanks a lot, Nora thought.

"Perhaps he could think of me as an honorary uncle?"

Nora sighed. He wasn't getting the idea at all. "Why not?" she said gloomily.

He gazed at her in silence for several seconds, then said out of the blue, "You know, Nora, the job here could still be yours if you want it." His pale blue eyes had brightened with enthusiasm as he spoke, and the twitch had disappeared completely. "If you like, we can talk over lunch about adjusting your hours," he added.

Nora's mood brightened dramatically. "We can? You're offering me the job anyway?"

He smiled indulgently. "How does Seminar Director sound?"

"Wonderful."

"Perhaps another thousand a month...."

Guilt was making him magnanimous. Nora sighed. Could she accept an offer based on guilt? Of course she couldn't. Even though she deserved the job. She was his best field representative, and she had labored long and hard on his behalf. Even though she deserved to take life a little easier, to stay home more . . .

"I can't take the job, John," she said with difficulty. "I'm morally incapable of forcing you to keep a promise that went hand in hand with your proposal. I wasn't going to accept, you see. I had decided that it just wouldn't work out—"

He was shaking his head, gripping her shoulder more tightly. "Thank you for trying to make everything easier for me, Nora. I should have known you would be nice about it. And strong. I appreciate what you are trying to do, I really do. And more than ever, I want you to have the promotion. I really need you in the head office. I've been too much the workaholic. Kate opened my eyes to that, too. I haven't allowed myself to have any fun. With you running things here, I, too, could take more time off, relax a little."

She couldn't imagine John ever really having fun, wasn't sure he knew how to, but she wasn't going to protest any more. She wanted the job, he wanted her to have the job. That was enough.

AN HOUR LATER she elbowed open the front door of her parents' house, juggling her attaché case, a half-empty magnum of Dom Perignon and a tiny jar of caviar— real caviar, not the cheap whitefish roe she normally passed off on guests—and called out, "Hey, Mom, Dad, is anyone up for a celebration?"

After treating her to champagne and Szechuan prawns in Chinatown—an unusual choice, and perhaps the start of the loosening-up process—her boss had given her the rest of the day off. She'd welcomed the suggestion wholeheartedly. She hadn't slept at all the previous night, wondering what she was going to do about Kerry Ryan. Once on her way home, though, she had realized she was much too excited and perhaps too tipsy to sleep. She rarely drank anything alcoholic and the champagne had gone straight to her head.

"Mom, Dad?" she called again, then sounded a cheery tattoo on the lion's-head knocker on their apartment door. No answer. Well, perhaps they were upstairs.

She had fumbled her own door open before she realized something was missing. Rusty. Usually he started barking the minute she entered the downstairs foyer.

Setting the bottle and jar down on the kitchen counter, she glanced at the cork bulletin board above the wall telephone to see if her mother had left a message. Nothing. She went swiftly through the apartment. No dog, no parents. Standing in her bedroom, she frowned, considering. Where would her parents go in the middle of a Monday afternoon? Wait a minute. Hadn't Lillian said something about Rusty needing some shots?

So. She was alone. And Gregory wouldn't be home from school for two-and-a-half hours. "Some celebration," she muttered.

A minute later, she decided this was no time to wallow in self-pity. She would celebrate by herself. Briskly, she walked into her kitchen and started boiling half-a-dozen eggs. When they were hard-cooked and she'd cooled them in ice water, she mashed them into a paste with half a stick of melted butter, spread them in a crystal dish, covered them with a thin layer of sour cream and chives and topped them with the precious caviar.

Next she changed into a pretty apricot satin robe her parents had given her for Christmas, arranged toast points around the spread and carried the platter, the Dom Perignon and a single champagne flute into the living room. She was struggling to remove the cork the waiter had replaced for her—after she and John had thoroughly toasted her new position—when the doorbell rang.

Probably the Avon lady, she decided, allowing some self-pity to creep back.

But it was Kerry Ryan, living up to his reputation for unpredictability. He was devastating in tan slacks and a white shirt and knitted tan tie and a navy-blue windbreaker, his hair untousled by ocean breezes, mustache neatly groomed. He looked as if he'd just walked out of the pages of *Gentleman's Quarterly.* "I happened to be in the neighborhood...." he began brightly, then did a comical double take and took a step backward. "They told me at your office that you'd gone home, but I had no idea this was how you spent your afternoons off."

She looked at him blankly, stunned by his unexpected arrival, then realized she was cradling the magnum of champagne as though it were a baby. "I was going to finish celebrating," she explained vaguely.

"Obviously."

His grin was contagious. She suddenly felt terrifically lighthearted, as though the bubbles in the champagne had exploded inside her. She grinned back at him. "What a nice surprise to see you."

He raised both eyebrows. "Does that mean you might invite me in eventually?"

Embarrassed, she backed away from the door and waved him inside with a flourish. He looked around. "No Rusty?"

Closing and locking the door, she frowned. "I guess Mom and Dad must have taken him to the vet's for shots. Mom didn't leave a note, which is unusual, but she does get absentminded sometimes."

"Gregory's in school?"

She nodded, preceding him into the kitchen. He was leading up to something, obviously, and she had the feeling she ought to say a few words first about her feelings, her objections to . . . what? Wasn't she angry with him about something? She leaned against the sink as he took the champagne bottle from her, and frowned at him, narrow-eyed. The trouble was that looking at him made pleasure suffuse her entire body and the champagne she'd drunk already had dulled her brain and she really couldn't remember. . . .

The cork popped and ricocheted from the ceiling, startling her. Kerry had opened the bottle without any apparent difficulty. There were some things that men were just able to do better, she decided vaguely.

"Glasses?" he prompted, and she realized she was still staring blankly at him, trying to remember.

She nodded, took a second flute from the liquor cabinet and led the way to the living room, where she gestured at her own glass and the toast and caviar. "Nice," he commented. "What are we celebrating?"

"I have a new job. Seminar director. I won't be on the road as much. I'll be home more for Gregory." She accepted a glass from him, took a sip of the sparkling contents and smiled ruefully. "I think John felt guilty because he'd jilted me. Shortest engagement on record."

He laughed. "Congratulations on both counts. I'm sure you deserve the job anyway."

"I do," she agreed.

"John called Mom this morning."

She nodded. "I know. He's really smitten, but he seems to accept that she's not seriously interested. He says he's going to loosen up, so I guess the whole experience was good for him."

"I thought it might be," he said, smirking.

"Yes, well, I'm still not so sure it was a good thing to do, but I guess it had the desired effect. I'm off the hook and I've got the job I wanted."

"So I'm completely forgiven?"

"I guess so."

There was a strain between them. She really ought to ask him. . . .

He was setting his glass down on the coffee table, taking her glass from her hand. She really couldn't remember sitting down on the sofa, but there she was . . . there they both were, side by side. He put his arm around her shoulders and pulled her in toward his body. "Kerry," she said tentatively, but he was suddenly so close to her that his features were blurring. "Kerry," she said again, softly this time.

"I came to ask you something," he said.

"Oh yes, you said last night you wanted to talk to me. Sounded ominous." She took a deep breath. "Ask away."

His lips brushed against hers. The champagne bubbles exploded again and his mustache tickled her upper lip. The combination made her giggle.

"I came to ask you to marry me," he murmured against her mouth.

Her head reared back and she must have stared at him for at least two minutes before she found her voice. "Are you *serious*?"

He looked offended. "Would I kid about something like that?"

"No, I guess you wouldn't." She stared at him. This couldn't possibly be happening, she thought woozily. She must have dreamed it. The champagne had put her to sleep, and she'd dreamed his arrival.

"Do you want me to list the benefits the way John did?" He inclined his head to one side and looked thoughtful. "Of course, the benefits in this case are pretty obvious. We have here a great-looking guy with a wonderful body. A secure financial future. Sex is no problem. You may have noticed that."

"I thought you were going to tell me we were through," she blurted out. "You've been behaving very strangely, Kerry. We didn't spend a minute alone at the lodge. You were avoiding me."

He nodded, not attempting to deny her accusation. "I was in a funk," he said.

"A what?"

He kissed her again, exerting more pressure this time. His arms were holding her very close. "A funk," he repeated. "A pusillanimous, cowardly, chicken-hearted, fraidy-cat funk. As soon as I realized that I was in love with you, that I was only happy when I was with you, that I wanted to paint window frames with you...."

"Do what?"

"I dreamed we were painting the window frames at the lodge. You and I. I never dreamed stuff like that about any other woman. And then after July 4, when I brought you here and then went back to the lodge for our family meeting, it was as if the color had all gone out of the place. The sea wasn't blue anymore and the sand wasn't golden."

"Everything turned gray," Nora murmured, remembering how San Francisco had looked to her in the fog.

He nodded. "It scared me to death for a while." He looked at her apologetically. "I wasn't sure I could settle down with only one woman, you see. But then something happened that made me decide I might just be ready for marriage after all. And then when I saw the look on my mother's face last night, I knew it for sure. I wanted some woman to look like that for me." He shook his head, evidently impatient with himself. "Not some woman, this woman," he said, hugging her. "At the same time I realized you probably wouldn't look like that about me until we'd been married eighteen years . . . which is how long my parents had before my father died. Eighteen years is a long time, so I thought we'd better get started on it." He paused for a breath and looked her in the eye. "I love you, Nora Courtney, and I have an idea you might love me too."

"I do, but—"

"But me no buts," he said sternly. "I don't want you to even think about it yet. I don't want any answer from you until we've examined *all* the benefits."

"But there's something I have to think about . . . I've been trying to think, I know there was a reason . . ." She was stammering because he had stood up and lifted her in his arms and was carrying her across the living room.

"I never did get to explore your bedroom," he said. He grinned down at her. "How much time do we have?"

"Gregory will come home in about two hours, but Mom and Dad will be home first, so he'll go down there. He won't be expecting me home until 5:30 or so."

"Wonderful." He sounded absentminded. He was looking at her platform bed and the Chinese screen on the wall behind it, the white enameled goosenecked floor lamp that arched over the headboard, the free-form white leather chair and ottoman in the corner near the window seat. "This stuff is not going to go with my Duncan Phyfe," he muttered as he crouched awkwardly to set her down on the bed.

"I can't marry you, Kerry," she blurted out, sitting up cross-legged on the oyster-satin comforter. "I can't go to live in Oregon. I told you, I have a new job."

He shook his head, knelt down beside her and began unfastening the buttons of her robe. "You can work for me," he said. "Let John Simpson Bradford loosen up by himself. I'm going to have several jobs available in the near future, so you won't have to worry about advertising skills. We're doing some expanding."

"But I like my new job. At least I will when I get started in it. And anyway, I can't leave San Francisco. This is my home. I told you. I can't imagine living anywhere else."

He had managed to get her robe off, and had removed his own jacket and shirt and tie. Now he eased her down on the bed and leaned over her, ducking his head down to kiss first one breast then the other. Sighing, relaxing his arms so that he was lying on top of her, he murmured, "I thought we were going to examine the benefits before reaching any decisions."

"But the fact remains that I can't leave here."

She was frowning, wrinkling her forehead in a way that he found adorable. To be honest, now that he'd broken down and allowed himself to admit he was in love and ready to get married, he was finding everything about Nora Courtney adorable, even the fact that she was suddenly exhibiting reluctance, when she was supposed to be the one who was the marrying kind. Her breasts were certainly adorable, small and firm and beautifully shaped. He leaned over to kiss them again.

"Kerry," she protested. "You're not listening to me. We have to discuss this."

Sighing again, he lifted his head. "There's no need for a discussion," he said with what he felt was commendable patience. "If you don't want to leave San Francisco, I'll have to come here. I'll just move my whole business into Oakland, merge the two plants."

She stared up at him in disbelief. "You'd do that for me?" Her voice was soft as a breeze through a country meadow.

He nodded. "Like a shot. Now can we get on with the benefits?"

"Oh, Kerry." Her face was suddenly radiant, her arms welcoming.

Never one to let opportunity pass by, he began kissing her very gently, his lips barely touching hers, then withdrawing, then touching again, tasting, tasting again. "Garlic?" he queried. "Chili?"

"Both, I'm afraid. The Pot Sticker makes this spicy sauce for their prawns. John took me to lunch there." There was apology in her voice. "Maybe I should go brush my teeth," she suggested. "I hadn't got around to that."

He held her tightly against him. "I love the taste of garlic and chili," he said staunchly.

She laughed. "Liar. Nothing tastes good second-hand."

"Is that so?" Ever ready to tease, he began a line of kisses that moved slowly downward and ended between her legs. "Everything about you tastes wonderful to me," he murmured. Her flesh was like satin, fragrant with perfume, dewy with perspiration—the soft triangle of brown hair was velvet against his lips.

"I love you, Nora," he murmured.

She lifted herself to his exploring tongue, sending shivers of sensation throughout his entire body. "I love you, Kerry," she gasped.

She had stopped worrying about his proposal, he realized. Whatever objections she had thought of had lost themselves in the passion that was beginning to grow between them. He kissed her lovingly, delicately, then with more force, timing kisses to the rhythm of her movements, reveling in the warmth of her loins, the lifting of her lower body as the joyous pressure mounted inside her. His hands stroked her, caressed her, encouraged her, then gathered her close to his side when the pressure exploded and she cried out in release. Giving her no time to come down, no time to think, he began kissing her breasts, teasing each nipple erect with his tongue, grazing the tender underside with his mustache, then trailing moist kisses upward over warm, silky flesh.

They made love to each other for a long time in the dim bedroom. Time had no meaning as they moved and stilled and moved again, kissing and stroking and touching and nibbling in all the ways they had ever experienced or heard of or read about or could invent on the spur of the moment.

"I can hear you purring," Kerry whispered against Nora's throat, surfacing for a breath of air.

She kissed the top of his head, then reached under his arms to pull him level with her. Her mouth searched for and found his and clung, her tongue gently probing as she continued to make the soft incoherent sound he had called purring, which wasn't really purring but was more like a soft whimper, reflecting her excitement and exciting him in turn.

His hand cupped her breast and he thought suddenly of the children she would bear, the children she would nurse, his children. His whole body seemed to melt with tenderness. She would breast-feed her children, he knew without asking. She was that kind of woman, an earth mother, loving and nurturing and fierce in her devotion.

As though she had read his thoughts, her hand covered his, trapping it in sweet imprisonment against her breast and she looked into his eyes, her own eyes dark with love and passion and wanting. "It's my turn to pleasure you again," she murmured.

"You only have to be to pleasure me," he said, then laughed softly. "I never said I was a poet."

She laughed with him. How wonderful to find a woman who could laugh with him.

A heartbeat and he stopped thinking about laughter, stopped thinking about anything but his own senses as her hands moved lower on his body and her mouth followed them down, touching, kissing, exploring, pressing here quite firmly, brushing over this area with tantalizing, gossamer kisses, her tongue touching there and there and there.

He felt as though he were surrounded by light. He could barely keep his eyes open because of the urgency of his body's hungers, but even so the impression of light was there, even though the vertical slats of the window blinds were closed tightly against the afternoon. Like a fireworks display, the light continued to flash and crackle even after he'd given in and closed his eyes, his whole concentration focused on that so sensitive part of his body that was receiving all of Nora's attention.

She had no foolish inhibitions, his Nora. His Nora. Odd how he'd known subconsciously, right at the start, that she was his Nora.

He felt as though he were floating now, levitating right up off the bed, hearing his heartbeat hammering in his ears, feeling his breath quickening, his fists clenching, his whole body stiffening in preparation . . .

But he didn't want to take this last journey alone. He wanted her beside him, entwined with him, part of him.

"Nora," he called urgently. She understood immediately, and climbed up over him. For just a moment she teased him, holding her body a bare millimeter above his. His hands were alongside his body, fingers curled tightly in his palms. Letting herself down onto his body, she teased his hands open with her fingertips, then placed her palms flat against his, letting him feel the difference in the size of their hands. The calluses beneath his fingers pressed against the tiny soft pillows beneath hers. Looking up into her eyes, restraining the impulse to thrust into her, roll over with her, he moved his thumbs instead, stroking the soft inner surfaces of her hands.

He heard the swift intake of her breath, saw her eyes glow, her lips part. He gathered her in then, and rolled with her and kissed her deeply and thoroughly as he entered her. Bracing himself above her on both hands, he covered her face and throat with kisses, his eyes wide open now, gazing at her as though afraid she might disappear if he looked away. He couldn't bear it if she disappeared.

She was murmuring his name now, over and over like a litany, a child's prayer against the dark. She was arching against him, lifting him, slender as she was and heavy as he was, lifting him with the force of her passion. She surrounded him, held him, and moved explosively with him at the exact moment that he climaxed. His body went rigid, then collapsed as the molten fire in his loins passed from his body to hers.

THE SHEETS AND PILLOWCASES on her bed were dark blue with little pyramids of beige dots patterning their surfaces. He was surprised. He would have thought they would be white, like the rest of her furnishings. A second look at the pillow beneath her sweat-dampened hair revived a memory of a familiar catalog. "Laura Ashley," he muttered.

"I hope you're talking about my designer sheets and not calling for some other woman," Nora said.

He laughed, and kissed her lightly. After two hours of lovemaking her mouth was moist, rosy and swollen with his kisses. "What other woman?" he said lazily. "There isn't any other woman in the whole world but Nora. Nora, Nora, Nora, your name is a song."

"Who says you're not a poet," she teased, then snuggled closer against him, loving the way his muscular body felt against the length of hers. "How come you know about Laura Ashley sheets?" she asked curiously.

She felt him shrug. "I know a lot about fabrics. Some toys require such knowledge. We did a dollhouse recently with all of its furniture upholstered in Laura Ashley fabrics. Pink and white. Gorgeous. Every one of my nieces wants one."

She frowned as something stirred in her memory. Something to do with fabrics. She couldn't think what it might be.

"HOW ABOUT SOME FLAT CHAMPAGNE?" Kerry asked as they knelt on either side of her platform bed, straightening the sheets and comforter. They had already showered and dressed, concerned that time was passing and it was possible that Gregory might decide to come upstairs to look through his telescope or work on his model airplane. So that none of her family would guess what they'd been up to, Nora had put on the creamy blouse and tailored linen skirt she'd worn earlier. At some point in the afternoon they had heard the downstairs door open and close. They had both tensed for a second, but neither Lillian nor Charlie had ventured up the stairs. After a while they had heard the sound of a television set down below.

Nora made a face. "We did leave the cork out, didn't we? After that nice Chinese waiter pressed it in for me, too. You should have seen him, Kerry, no more than five feet tall but strong as a horse. He said he was an expert in kung fu." She laughed. "John was very interested. He said he might take lessons. Did I tell you he's going to change his life-style? All Kate's doing."

She glanced at him as she smoothed the oyster satin comforter in place. He had stood up and was looking down at her, watching her with a bemused expression on his face. "You aren't even listening to me, are you?" she accused.

He smiled, gazing at her with so much love that her breath caught in her throat. "I'm listening," he said. "I was just thinking about things, such as how very much I love you."

"I love you too, Kerry Ryan."

He raised his eyebrows. "Is your heart bouncing in your chest?"

"Like Silly Putty."

He looked horrified. "Don't say that," he rasped. "That's a rival company."

They both laughed, then he came around the bed to her and offered his hand to help her to her feet. Putting his arms around her, he held her comfortably against him. She liked the feeling of being held after all the demands of sex had been satisfied. She felt warm and safe.

"What else were you thinking?" she asked.

"You never did say you'd marry me."

"You said I should think it over," she reminded him.

"But if you were really anxious you'd shout out yes, yes, yes."

"I wasn't sure about where we were going to live. Now that you've settled that, I can shout yes, yes, yes." She frowned. "Are you sure, Kerry, about moving the whole plant to Oakland, just for me? That's the most remarkably generous thing I've ever heard of, but don't you have to consult your sisters and their husbands and your mother. . . ."

The skin at the corners of his eyes crinkled as he smiled guiltily. "I guess I didn't quite tell you the whole story there."

She eyed him suspiciously. "Maybe you'd better tell me now."

"Uh-huh." He took a deep breath, dropped a kiss on her nose and said, "Well, we decided to expand some time ago. We couldn't decide whether to rebuild in Oregon—the original plant is falling apart—or to add on to the factory in Oakland. We decided it made more sense financially to add on here. Roy wanted us to go public to help finance the change, but we decided instead to let the employees buy stock so the business would still be in the family, so to speak."

"This is what all your meetings were about?"

"Yes. We made the final decisions at our family conference right after July 4 and started the ball rolling last week. Jordan and Bridget and Kate and I have been talking to the money men, and it looks as though it's going to work out very well."

She gave him a glance of mock exasperation. "So the decision to relocate had nothing to do with me at all."

"Well, not really," he admitted, but when she said, "Just as I thought," he went on to say that he'd been leaning toward Oregon until she said she'd never leave San Francisco and then he'd found himself leaning toward San Francisco. "That's when I knew I was in trouble," he said with a grin.

She looked at him curiously. "What exactly did turn the tide?" she asked. "What made you decide you were ready for marriage? You said something happened."

Looking a little embarrassed, he took his arms from around her waist and suggested they go in search of the flat champagne and caviar, he was really getting rather hungry. Nora went along with the suggestion, but after they were seated on the sofa and he'd inhaled several pieces of toast and pronounced the spread delicious, she returned to the subject. "Come on, Kerry," she urged. "You were definitely set against marriage. What changed your mind?"

"It wasn't a what, it was a who," he said obscurely.

"Who then? Kate? Bridget?"

"A woman called Greta Mallory," he said.

She jumped to her feet, almost spilling her champagne. Carefully setting the glass down on the coffee table, she glared at him. "I almost forgot," she said. "The champagne made things a bit fuzzy and then I was so busy thinking about getting promoted and getting married to you and how great everything was, I almost forgot about Greta Mallory."

He looked astonished. "You know Greta?"

The telephone rang. "We'll finish this discussion in a minute," Nora said tightly, then ran for the phone.

"Nora, dear," her mother said into her ear. "I'm sorry to bother you but I just wanted to double-check. Gregory *is* up there, isn't he?"

Nora's blood ran cold. It was a moment before she could find her voice. Then it came out as a squeak. "You're telling me he's not there?"

"Oh dear," Lillian said.

"Do you have Rusty?"

"No. No, we don't." Lillian sounded terribly alarmed. "I left him upstairs in Gregory's room with his bed and some food and water. Your father heard about this antique show in Berkeley, you see, and he thought he'd check it out. He's trying to find an umbrella stand for the foyer. And then we had lunch at that pub he likes so much and . . . but darling, we were home in plenty of time for Gregory. We saw your car but we didn't come up because we saw Kerry's car also." She broke off, then spoke again before Nora could get a word in. "Rusty isn't there either? You looked everywhere?"

"Of course I looked everywhere. Mom, think now, did Gregory have anything going on after school?"

"No, dear. He would have told me. Maybe something came up at the last minute."

"But that wouldn't explain Rusty's absence. What time did you and Dad leave?"

There was the sound of a discussion, then Lillian came back on the line. "Around eleven, dear."

"I came home at two and Rusty was gone then, so evidently some time between eleven and two Gregory came home and got him. Probably during his lunch break."

"Why would he do that, dear?"

"I have no idea, Mom. At any rate, he ought to be home by now, whether he has Rusty with him or not." She paused, considering. Kerry was standing nearby, watching her alertly, obviously following the conversation closely. "Kerry and I will go check the school," she continued into the phone. "Maybe you or Dad could come up here in case he calls this number."

"How late is he?" Kerry asked when she hung up.

She glanced at her wristwatch as she hurried into the bedroom to get her suit jacket. Kerry followed her, pulling on his windbreaker. "Only half an hour, but it's not like him. And where could Rusty be? I took it for granted Mom had taken him somewhere, but Gregory must have come home and—" She stopped dead halfway into her jacket and looked desperately at Kerry, feeling stricken. "You don't suppose he got out of school early and took Rusty for a walk in the park? There are all kinds of crazies in this city. . ."

"Unfortunately there are crazies in every city," Kerry said, "but there's no sense thinking the worst. Prob-

ably he just decided to take Rusty out and lost track of
the time."

"But it's not like him."

"We all do things unlike ourselves from time to time.
We're going to check the school first?"

"Yes." She was searching her handbag, trying to find
her car keys but her hands were shaking so badly she
couldn't keep hold of anything.

"I'll drive," Kerry said, taking her elbow and easing
her toward the door.

Nora looked at him gratefully. "I'm sorry, Kerry,
usually I stay calm in emergencies, but Gregory is so,
he's everything . . . well, I just love him so much."

"I know."

Running downstairs, they met Charlie on his way up
to sit by Nora's phone. He looked very tight-lipped and
pale. "You'll call when you find him?" he asked as they
went by.

"Of course we will, Dad."

"We never should have stayed out so long."

"You mustn't blame yourself," Nora said, turning at
the foot of the stairs. "Gregory was supposed to be in
school. This just isn't like him," she said again to Kerry.

"We'll find him," he soothed as he opened the front
door.

But they didn't find him, and after a while even Kerry
began to look anxious. They began at the school, which
was a fifteen minute drive from the Courtney house.
Everyone had left for the day except a secretary and the
janitor, neither of whom could shed any light on Gregory's whereabouts. School had closed at the regular

time, the secretary informed them. The minibuses that took the children to their homes had left on schedule. No, she hadn't seen Gregory or anyone else, she had been in the multi-purpose room all afternoon, helping with some decorations for the end-of-term party, due to take place in another week. But she had heard the buses pull out. No, she hadn't seen a dog anywhere.

Nora called home to make sure Gregory and Rusty hadn't turned up. They hadn't.

"We have to think like an eight-year-old," Kerry said when they were back in his car. "A very, very bright eight-year-old. Where does Gregory like to go?"

"The Exploratorium," Nora said, biting her lip. "Fisherman's Wharf, The Embarcadero, The Coit Tower for the view, The Planetarium." She broke off. "There are only so many places he could take a dog. He couldn't take a bus or a cable car with Rusty, or a train either. He's a terrific walker, though, he did twenty-two miles in the last March of Dimes Walkathon." She looked at Kerry, suddenly feeling frantic. "You don't think Nathan would come and get him, take him away, hide him from me? Divorced fathers do that all the time."

"Nathan's never even tried to see Gregory, has he?"

She shook her head.

"If he did get interested, he would surely talk about visitation rights first, don't you think?"

"I suppose so. I'm sorry, Kerry, I'm not thinking straight, I guess."

He put his arm around her shoulders as he drove, and held her close. "We'll find him," he said again with so much confidence that she was suddenly convinced that they would.

They began with the Embarcadero Center because it wasn't too far from Gregory's school. They checked the entire five-block complex, including the lobby of the Hyatt Regency, because Gregory loved its spectacular architecture and fabulous skylighted central court.

At Fisherman's Wharf they separated to make the search more efficient, but trying to find a small boy and a dog among all the tourists was almost impossible. Ghirardelli Square and The Cannery were every bit as crowded. Gregory's school might still be in session, but most schools in the nation weren't, and it began to seem to Nora that the pupils from all those schools had descended en masse on San Francisco.

Time and again, as she hurried along on foot, trying to push through a mass of happy holiday-making people who didn't care whether they were in her way, feeling as though she was locked in a nightmare, she would catch sight of a dark head of hair and her heart would ricochet against her ribs. But the child would turn out to wear glasses or have Oriental features. "Please God," she found herself begging under her breath.

"Let's make one more pass on the roads leading to your house," Kerry suggested when they met once more at his car. "If we don't see him, I think we'd better call the police."

Nora nodded, taking a deep breath, trying to stay calm because giving in to panic wasn't going to help anything, but somehow just the thought of going to the police made Gregory's disappearance more serious, more real. As they drove homeward, her imagination produced vivid and terrible pictures of small blood-stained bodies, of pictures flashed on television with captions begging, "Have you seen this child?" If she didn't find Gregory, if anything had happened to Gregory, she would never recover from the agony of it. "Please God," she muttered again and again.

And then she saw him.

He was toiling up the hill a few yards ahead of them with Rusty in his arms. He had on his school back-pack, full of books as usual, and he was moving very slowly as though his feet hurt.

Kerry stamped on the brakes the second she screeched "There he is," but Nora was out of the car and running up the hill, calling, "Gregory!" at the top of her voice before the wheels stopped turning.

She crouched when she reached them and drew boy and dog into her arms, hugging and berating her son at the same time, tears streaming down her face.

"I'll go ahead and tell Lillian and Charlie he's safe," Kerry said, driving up alongside.

Nora flashed him a look of gratitude through her tears, still holding tightly to her son.

"Don't forget to turn your wheels in," Gregory called.

Kerry laughed and nodded and drove on up the hill.

"Where on earth have you been?" Nora demanded. "I've been scared to death. You didn't call, you didn't leave a note. When did you get Rusty, how did you get Rusty? Did you play hooky from school?"

"It's a long story," Gregory said.

"Tell me," Nora demanded, not letting go of him. She could feel his thin arms clinging tightly to her and knew he had been as frightened as she, though he might never admit it.

"Could we wait until I go to the bathroom and get some milk or something, and maybe sit down?" Gregory asked in a wavering voice.

Nora let go of him so she could blow her nose. She had managed to stop crying, and now that she could see Gregory clearly she realized that he was looking very frazzled. "Is everything A-okay?" she asked in their private code.

"Not really," he said with a sigh.

Nora grabbed his arms. "Did anybody. . . did someone try to hurt you or . . ."

"I'm fine, Mom, just tired," he assured her. "I walked from clear over the other side of Market."

"Gregory! What were you doing there?"

He grinned, looking suddenly delighted with himself. "I was visiting my friend Harvey Blassingame."

"IT WAS KERRY'S IDEA," Gregory said. He was sitting in his grandparents' living room on the uncomfortable antique sofa that Charlie insisted on keeping because of its French medallion back.

"It wasn't his fault," he added hastily when Nora, Lillian and Charlie all turned to glare at Kerry.

He took a gulp of milk, rubbed the bridge of his nose where the freckles congregated and grinned at Kerry. "You remember I told you about Harvey?"

"The bully."

"That's him. You said I should do something nice for him, be so nice he wouldn't want to get mad at me. And it's been working right along, most of the time. Cookies here and there, some of Gran's brownies. This morning, he wasn't in a good mood and he started picking on me, like out of habit, you know, so to distract him, I told him about Rusty and what a smart dog he is." He sighed. "He kept acting like he didn't believe I had a dog, so I said I'd take a bus home at lunchtime and get Rusty and take him to school. Which is what I did." He glanced at his mother, "I got permission from Ms Ellison." He hesitated, looking guilty. "She didn't know you weren't driving me back though."

"That was a long walk right there," Charlie commented.

"You can say that again," Gregory said with feeling. "Halfway to school Rusty sat down and wouldn't move. I had to carry him the rest of the way."

They all looked at Rusty, who was curled up on the bed Gregory had insisted be brought down for him. One floppy ear covered the dog's eyes as though to keep out the light. He was snoring faintly.

"Anyway," Gregory went on. "It worked out okay. Harvey was real impressed that I would come all this way and go back again just to show him my dog. We swore a vow of eternal friendship and he promised to stop picking on me. But then he begged, absolutely begged me to take the school bus to his house so his dad could see Rusty and maybe get Harvey a dog just like him. So what could I do?"

"You could have called home," Charlie said.

"I didn't think anyone was home yet," Gregory pointed out. "Gran told me you'd be gone most of the day, and I knew Mom wouldn't be here. I figured I'd probably beat everyone home, anyway. I thought someone would drive me home from his house. Shows what a dummy I was. I didn't know his family was really poor. He's in my school on a scholarship because he's such a brain." He looked at his mother, his eyes wide. "They have two little rooms for four people, Mom. Really clean—Harvey's mom sees to that— but so small. They do have a little backyard, though, so Harvey had this idea they could build a kennel and have a dog there." He sighed. "Well, Harvey's dad put the kibosh on that. He said dogs like Rusty were very expensive." He glanced at Kerry. "Is that right?"

Kerry nodded.

"So Harvey was real disappointed," Gregory continued. "But I told him he can come here and play with Rusty sometimes. Is that okay, Mom?"

"Sure it is, sport," Nora said. "But I still don't understand why you didn't let us know where you were. We'd have come to get you."

"Well, I guess I never did get to that," he said. "I told you Harvey's folks were pretty poor, but I didn't tell you they don't even have a phone. I didn't have any money for a public phone, and I didn't want to ask them for money, considering they don't have so much, so I thought I'd just better walk home. So that's what I did."

"You might have gotten lost," his grandfather exclaimed.

"I've seen a map of San Francisco," Gregory said indignantly. Nora laughed, knowing that her son could recall in absolute detail anything he'd once studied. She could imagine him trudging along, now and then consulting the grid of streets laid out in his brain.

"Harvey's father shouldn't have let you walk all that way alone," Charles said, determined to keep worrying even though the panic was over.

"Well, he offered to come with me," Gregory explained. "But he doesn't have a car, they had to sell it when he got laid off. It wasn't his fault he got laid off, he's a real nice guy and all that, but his job came to an end because the company closed down. There's a lot of that going on, he said. His dad tries real hard, Harvey says, but he just can't seem to get on his feet." He shook his head, his brow furrowed. "I can sure see why Harvey gets mad about things," he said to Nora. "I'd get mad at people if I had to live in that little apartment all the time." He sighed deeply. "Anyway, Harvey's dad had been out looking for a job all day and he was pretty beat, so I told him I'd call you from the first phone I saw. I knew I couldn't do that, so technically that was a lie, but I didn't want him dragging out, you know."

"What kind of work is he looking for?" Kerry asked.

Gregory's brow wrinkled. "General laboring, I guess. Things are tough everywhere, he says. Not too many buildings going up."

"How about if I give you one of my business cards to give Harvey's dad," Kerry suggested. "I'm going to be hiring quite a few people."

Gregory's grin threatened to split his face. "Hey, that would be great."

"And I also know where Harvey can get a dog like Rusty for free, just as soon as he has a place suitable to keep him and his dad says it's okay," Kerry added.

"You'd give him one of your dogs?" Gregory's eyes were suddenly moist. So were Nora's.

"That's awfully nice of you, Kerry," she said.

"I'm feeling nice today," he told her with a grin. "Nice things were happening all around until Gregory turned up missing."

Her eyes flashed a warning at him, she'd *told* him her father could pick up on double entendres, but he simply grinned again.

"What's going on?" Charlie asked, immediately alert.

"I'm glad you asked, Charlie," Kerry said. He leaned forward on his chair, smiling, obviously prepared to tell all.

"It's a long story, Dad," Nora interrupted. "Gregory's pooped and needs to have his supper and go to bed early. Then Kerry and I have to have a few words before making any announcements."

"We do?" Kerry queried, looking innocently puzzled. "What about?"

"About Greta Mallory."

The innocence was replaced by a smirk. "Oh."

"Exactly," Nora said.

"There's going to be an announcement?" Lillian asked.

"Maybe," Nora glanced over at Gregory to see how her son was taking these vague hints and saw that he had flopped down on the sofa, one arm across his eyes in unconscious imitation of his dog.

"I'll carry him up," Kerry offered, getting to his feet.

"We aren't going to get any announcement about you and Kerry?" Charlie asked, sounding disappointed.

"Tomorrow," Nora replied. "If it works out. For now it's enough for you to know that I've turned John down but he's given me a job at head office anyway, so I'll be around a lot more."

"That's great," Gregory murmured sleepily from Kerry's arms. His hands were clasped at the back of Kerry's neck, his head tucked confidingly into Kerry's shoulder. It was obvious that he felt very comfortable with Kerry.

"I'm so glad, dear," Lillian said, hugging her daughter. "About everything."

"So am I," Charlie said. Then he had to have a hug too. "I'm mighty glad I'm not getting John Simpson Bradford for a son-in-law."

"You think that would be bad," Kerry added from the doorway, pausing with Gregory in his arms. "I came close to getting him as a stepfather."

Charlie laughed. "You mean to tell me he fell for Kate? Of course your mom *is* a looker," he added with a sly glance at his wife. Lillian made a face at him.

"I LIKE YOUR PARENTS," Kerry said. "Salt of the earth."

A half hour had passed. Gregory had slept through the removal of his clothes and was tucked safely in bed, with Rusty on one side and the stargazing tiger on the other. Kerry and Nora had finished up the toast and caviar spread and poured the rest of the extremely flat champagne down the sink. They had decided to fix a hamburger apiece when they got through with their "discussion."

"Mom and Dad like you too," Nora said, leaning back on the couch and kicking off her shoes so she could wiggle her toes. She had covered a lot of ground today. "They are wonderful people. I couldn't have managed all these years without them. I also like your whole family," she added. "However, you should know that the twins are inclined to gossip without checking if anyone's within hearing range."

He affected a wise expression. "Ah, that's how you knew about Greta."

"You are going to explain her, aren't you?"

"You don't trust me?"

"Not for a second."

He laughed. "Okay, I'll explain. Greta Mallory is a fabrics expert."

"Specializing in bear rugs in front of the fire."

"If you've already heard the story, why am I telling it?"

"I'm waiting for the sequel."

"Then quit interrupting." He leaned over and kissed her lightly, then took her hand and held it in his. What a lot of feeling could come through a hand, Nora thought. She could feel warmth in every vein, every capillary. . .

"Greta Mallory invented a material that is so close to fur it's incredible," Kerry said. "It can be dyed any color, but it's just as beautiful in its 'natural' state, which is pure white." He glanced at her sideways. "And yes, she did spread the first rug out in front of her fireplace and invited me to try it out. But being a virtuous person, I turned her down, even though I'm also a thoughtful person and hate to disappoint people."

"Brenda and Molly didn't think you turned her down."

"Brenda and Molly prefer to think the worst. So do my brothers-in-law. It made a better story, from their way of thinking, if I *did* tumble Greta Mallory on the rug." He put an arm around her shoulders and deposited a kiss on her forehead. "If we are going to be happily married, Nora darling, you must swear never to believe anything my sisters and their husbands tell you without checking with me first. They've all kissed the Blarney stone."

Nora laughed. "Okay," she promised. "But I'm still waiting for the sequel."

"I will admit," he continued, with one of his devilish smiles, "that I didn't turn Greta down immediately. I thought her offer over for at least five minutes, and I said no not because I have anything against female aggressiveness, but because I prefer a more subtle approach. To be truthful, I was very, very tempted. Sweating. Gasping for air."

Nora wondered if he was preparing her for something. She suddenly felt very cold. Was he going to tell her that the second time around he had succumbed to Greta's charms?

"However," Kerry said, looking at her narrow-eyed as though he knew exactly what she was thinking. "I managed to achieve heroic self-control and told Greta if she'd put her clothes on I'd take her out for a hot dog. She did, and we did. I might add that I spent months kicking myself for passing up such a terrific opportunity. And then, six months later, she turned up at the plant, at my office door to be precise."

"And?" Nora prompted when he hesitated.

He hesitated a moment more. "You must understand, Nora," he said finally, "that Greta is a very sexy lady. As I said, I hadn't seen her for six months though we'd talked often on the phone. When I heard she was there I was pretty sure my goose was cooked, unless she'd become remarkably ugly in the meantime. However," he continued with a smirk, "if anything her looks had improved." He had a smile of reminiscence on his face that Nora was tempted to slap away. He *was* preparing her for something, she was sure.

"Picture this," he said, putting his arm around her shoulders again, apparently not noticing how stiffly she was sitting. "I walk into my office and Greta is sitting in my office chair—one of those big leather jobs. She is very blond, very... how shall I put it... very curvaceous. She has her legs crossed and she's leaning back. Her hair has fallen over one eye... it's long and straight—the hair, not the eye. She is wearing, now get this, she is wearing a black lace top like what's her name—Madonna—and skinny-legged pants made of silk printed with leopard spots, with a brilliant blue raw-silk jacket over the lot, shoulders out to here, and black pumps with five-inch heels."

He'd certainly absorbed all the details. He was looking at her now as though to gauge her reaction.

"She sounds spectacular," Nora said stiffly.

"Spectacular?" He frowned, considering. "Nora, spectacular doesn't begin to describe this woman. She is sex personified. Wonderwoman, Marilyn Monroe, Dolly Parton, all rolled in one luscious bundle. And get this," he added, brightening, "the first thing she said to me was, 'Shall we start in where we didn't leave off?'" He looked at her in triumph. "Now I ask you, is that an invitation or not?"

"It certainly sounds like one."

"That's what I thought." He was still looking directly into her face, still with that irritatingly triumphant expression. "What you have to understand, Nora," he said, "is that I looked at this beautiful woman, this wonderful, gorgeous sex goddess, knowing she was mine for the asking . . . and do you know what I felt?"

"I have no idea." If he sang any more paeans of praise to Greta Mallory she was going to slap his face, she really was.

"Nothing," he said. "Nada, nil, zilch, zero."

He sat back, looking as delighted with himself as Gregory had looked earlier.

It was a minute before she registered what he'd said. "Nothing?" she echoed.

"Nothing." He reached for her, pulled her close and kissed her tenderly, thoroughly. "So you see," he said when he came up for air. "I knew then. If I could look at Greta Mallory and feel absolutely nothing, then either I was terminally ill or I had fallen in love. After Greta left in a huff I looked in the mirror and I seemed to be in fantastically good health, eyes bright, mustache perky as all get out, nose cool and all that. So evidently I was in love. You were the only female person I'd seen much of recently so it seemed logical to assume I was in love with you. And also logical that if I was that much in love, I was probably ready for marriage."

He leaned his head back and looked at her. "What do you think of that?"

"One of your better stories," she said judiciously.

"You do believe that nothing happened between me and Greta Mallory?"

"Absolutely."

"And you'll marry me and live happily ever after?"

"Yes." She smiled at him. "That's guaranteed? The happy ending?"

"There won't be an ending."

His arms tightened around her and his mouth brushed against hers, gently at first, then ardently, passionately. Nora's response was just as ardent. Somewhere, distantly, she heard the sound of a siren, the slam of a door, a foghorn, the wind rattling the branches of Lillian's favorite cypress tree against the window. There was something very comforting and comfortable about the sounds, even if they did seem far away and remote, like the background music in a movie that was compelling enough and dramatic enough to make the nature of the music unimportant.

After a while, Kerry stood and took her hand, suggesting they adjourn to the bedroom. "I have a project for us to work on," he told her.

She looked up at him, loving the devilishly wicked grin that so often came over his cheerfully friendly face. "What is it?" she asked, "A sequel to the matchmaker game?"

He did an exaggerated double take. "You guessed! How clever of you!" Sweeping her up in his arms, he carried her into her bedroom. "I'm going to call it Playing For Keeps." He deposited her carefully on her bed. "Will you research it with me?" He wasn't laughing now. His green eyes were completely serious.

Nora took a deep breath. "I will," she vowed.

Harlequin Temptation

COMING NEXT MONTH

ATTRACTIVE, SPACE SAVING BOOK RACK

Display your most prized novels on this handsome and sturdy book rack. The hand-rubbed walnut finish will blend into your library decor with quiet elegance, providing a practical organizer for your favorite hard-or soft-covered books.

Only $9.95

Approximately 16" x 8" when assembled

Assembles in seconds!

To order, rush your name, address and zip code, along with a check or money order for $10.70* ($9.95 plus 75¢ postage and handling) payable to *Harlequin Reader Service*:

All men wanted her,
but only one man would have her.

Desert Storm

Nan Ryan

Her cruel father had intended
Angie to marry a sinister cattle baron twice her age.
No one expected that she would fall in love with his
handsome, pleasure-loving cowboy son.

Theirs was a love no desert storm would quench.